The Only Way To Survive Is To
Be Prepared To Kill

BY

DAVID DOWSON

PROLOGUE

IN THE DEPTHS OF A VAST warehouse, the air hung heavy with anticipation, punctuated by the faint hum of flickering fluorescent lights. Three young boys, their faces etched with a volatile mix of excitement and shards of fear, stood amidst stacks of crates, clutching tightly to the drug consignment they intended to sell. Their naive ambition had led them down a path riddled with danger and deceit.

Drug pushing at fifteen.

As minutes stretched into an eternity, their youthful enthusiasm began to wane, replaced by an unsettling unease. The drug dealer they had been eagerly awaiting remained a phantom, his overdue presence becoming but a phantom in their minds. Doubt gnawed at their resolve, but desperation pushed them further into the clutches of the illicit underworld.*He'll come. We'll wait.*

Abruptly, the silence shattered like shards of glass. It was altered by the growing sound of heavy footsteps reverberating against the cold, concrete floor. From the shadows emerged a figure — the silhouette of something more formidable and, perhaps, with hidden intent. A cloak of darkness concealed his identity, and he exuded an aura of power and fearlessness that froze the boys in their tracks.

They knew that what was aheadwasn't their buyer. *What the hell is it then?* They wondered.

Instinct and survival propelled the boys into action. Theycouldn't hold back anymore. Panic gripped their trembling hands as they raised their weapons, desperation fueling their trigger fingers.

They unleashed fire. Their eyelids shut tight and their lips pressed against each other as their fingers remained on the trigger.

Gunfire erupted, filling the cavernous space with a symphony of chaos and danger. But their fears shut up when it seemed like the figure was unmoved by their strikes. He must be a ghost dancing between the hailstorm of bullets with unblemished grace.

With a fluidity that defied mortal limits, the man closed the distance between them, his movements a haunting ballet of dominance. He disarmed one of the boys with chilling ease, wrenching the weapon from his grasp. As the boy sprawled on the floor, begging to be spared, he said nothing but watched him beg in whispers, screams and moans.

Maybe, he was some psycho. Perhaps, the wails made him torture the boy the most. Alas! He pulled a gun from his black leather jacket — a 45 blowback pistol.

He stopped theboy's movement by stepping on one of his hands. The boy gnawed in pain. Thatdidn't move the man an inch.

He glanced at the boy who occasionally sprinkled his pleas with Spanish.
"Not everyone deserves mercy", he grumbled, unleashing a shot into theboy's head. His blood painted the ground red and spilt like the overspill of excessive paint.

The remaining two boys grew edgy and struck by terror. Before their very eyes, the man blew up the head of one of them.
He's a deadly murderer.
He's worth getting away from.

Despite their endless firing, the man possessed an aura of invincibility. One minute, he was in sight. The next minute, he was nowhere to be found. He tricked the boys, evading the onslaught of bullets with just sleek peek-a-boos that quickly came off as supernatural agility to the boys.

Their futile resistance crumbled beneath the weight of theman's unstoppable force, their pleas for mercy swallowed by the echoes of their futility.

He probablydidn't understand what mercy meant. As the second boy tripped over a bunch of wires on the floor, the other leapt away, leaving him to try entangling himself from the wires before the man could cover up the distance between them.

He was helpless; his Glock was out of bullets.

The warehouse became a canvas of tragedy, painted in the blood of broken dreams. Theman's lethal intent climaxed as he executed his merciless judgment. He gave the second boy a gun to shoot him, but the gun was empty. The stutter hit the air as the boy struck the trigger, his eyes melting in disappointment and fear.

He was brave. He wanted the ghost-looking man dead at all costs. Probably, he hated him. He had ruined their trade and was now after their lives, their youthful aspirations shattered in the face of a merciless reality.

"Not everyone deserves merc", the figure grumbled before putting a bullet in the secondboy's head.

With the terror and dead bodies already on the ground, the figure got so easy to get to the last boy standing. He was stuck near a lower stack of crates, his heart weak and legs watery. Hecouldn't try escaping anymore.

It took only a matter of a minute for the man to resurface. He lurched ahead towards the boy.

But fate, in its preemptive nature, interjected with a glimmer of hope right out of the blues. As the figure finally made to strike the only surviving boy, a sudden burst of activity seized the stagnant air. A special operations team burst through the doors, their arrival a crescendo of chaos and rescue.

Right on time!

His mission was incomplete as teargas grenades exploded and acrid fumes filled the warehouse, perfectly retreating the figure into the shadows.

Coughing and disoriented, the remaining boy stumbled through the haze, guided by the voices of the special ops team. Their arrival had snatched him from the jaws of certain death, but the scars of the harrowing encounter would forever mar his psyche.

In the aftermath, the warehouse stood as a silent witness, bearing the weight of unspeakable tragedy.

The law had the boy.

The murderercouldn't have him.

CHAPTER ONE

THE NIGHT WAS TRAPPED IN SILENCE.
UntilBancroft's sputters stabbed it. His sleep-driven body jerked into motion. His eyes snapped open, widening in alarm as a vice-like grip constricted around his throat.

Fierce. Solid. Strangling.

The room plunged into darkness, shadows coiling like serpents around his bed. His heart hammered against his chest, and each beat echoed in his ears like a war drum.

Have my nightmares grown hands now?

Instinct and adrenaline surged throughBancroft's veins, his survival instincts honed by years of rigorous training at American Navy camps. Groaning, he fought against the unknown hands dipping him deeper into the sinking bed with desperate fervour, his body becoming a vessel of furious power — he was getting adrenaline-drunk.

The scent of sweat mingled with the metallic tang of fear as he unleashed a barrage of punches and kicks, each strike driven by sheer determination to break out of the strangling chokehold.

He's got company.

One whodoesn't seem unfamiliar with sapping life out of people—one who might not want to leave until somebody is down in death.

Moonlight seeped through the grey curtains, casting low beams that danced upon the chaos. The room became a battleground, the air filled with the thud of blows colliding with flesh and bones cracking in a sickening symphony.Bancroft's powerful strikes reverberated through the room. Their impact ebbed with grunts as the attacker gasped in pain.

A few seconds after reeling fromBancroft's hard punch to his ribs, theattacker's silhouette emerged from the dark bend close to the coat standhe's a phantom figure whose features remain obscured. He flickered and blurred, becoming a mirage of fury. Oblivious of his angst, Bancroft pressed forward, unyielding in his assault, his senses alive with anticipation.

Hecan't wait to assault him in return!

Bancroft had him in his grip this time. Nothing would make him let him go. Determined to suck his life out, Bancroft groaned and gritted his teeth as his sturdy hands enveloped theattacker's broad neck—fierce and unrelenting like the grip of a starving Malaysian reticulated python.

With a burst of strength, Bancroft never saw from a distance. The figure broke free fromBancroft's grip, hurtling himself to the side of the bed in a loud stud. At the expense of three steps, Bancroft's outstretched arms smashed the switch on the wall, bringing up the light, shooing off the darkness that once lingered above them.

The light murdered the darkness and swallowed the tension as both men gawked at each other in deadpan silence.

Bancroftwouldn't back out. He was never trained to miss chances.

Clumsily and with an aching rib, Bancroft studied the figure closely as they both made a circle, calculating when and how best to strike again.

The figure's choice of cloth must have been carefully chosen. It reeked of stealthiest and came off quite flexible — little wonder it was dark enough to blend with the pitch darkness in the room. A black leather jacket with prominent water-resistant and lightweight properties is at the uppermost part of his trunk. It bore a subtle copper-thorn padding by the ribs and shoulders, suggesting protection without sacrificing agility and speed.

Only an assassin can be sophisticated in dressing. Bancroft's eyes didn't go off the figure an inch, and it was all out to scan through him with a fine-tooth comb. Underneath the jacket, the figure wore a close-fitting, high-performance black shirt that clung to his muscular physique like thick skin. It reminded Bancroft of the tan moisture-wicking, short-sleeved T-shirt he overused at his Land Warfare training at the Navy. The fabric showed off the figure's well-defined form like a stripper giving her best moves, accentuating the chiselled contours of his body. With his entire outward look, Bancroft was sure that every movement of his must have elicited a faint rustle of fabric, barely audible, as he navigated through the darkness with silent precision.

Completing the attacker's ensemble were lightweight, all-black combat boots, their soles designed to provide optimal traction and stability on any terrain. The boots allowed for near-silent movement, enabling him to glide stealthily through the darkest environments. It reminded Bancroft so much of his service years with the Navy SEAL and, at the same time, brimmed his head with questions with no answer at sight.

Bancroft's only hope of getting a glimpse of his attacker was his face, but the mask over it wouldn't let him see anything other than the dark eyes flickering behind it. It is a silicone mask moulded to his face with precision.

Damning his intimidating aura, Bancroft spiralled towards him like a pipped baboon. The figure's sleek moves got him close to a dodge, but Bancroft's arms swept him aside as they spun towards the wall, crashing into the human-length mirror in a loud stud.

No way out!

The mirror's glass shattered like a shower of crystal rain, tinkling melodies of destruction. Shards flew across the room, colliding with the tiled floor in clatters.

As always, Bancroft was fast but not fast enough. The figure jerked his frame up swiftly as if nothing had happened. Bancroft's next kick was supposed to knock the air out of him, but it knocked wholeness out of the flower vase on the table. With speed Bancroft couldn't detect, the figure headbutted Bancroft and volleyed his padded knees right into his midsection, and Bancroft slumped to the ground limbless.

Unrelenting, Bancroft shot a sized stool in this direction but crashed the window, opening a more comfortable getaway for the attacker. They both moved simultaneously but he had a better plan. He rifled a can of pepper spray off his belt and soaked Bancroft's face with it!

He sealed his defeat!

Bancroft groaned and moaned in excruciating pain, his jerky-trembling hands scraping his eyes like he was trying to absorb the potency of the spray.

Shit!

He thought that was it! And that was it. The figure snuck through the broken window and dashed into the heart of the night, leaving Bancroft in sheer pain.

Collapsing onto the bed, Bancroft gasped for breath, his chest heaving with the desperate need for oxygen. The spray had gone beyond his eyes and right into his auricles — it bubbled within his bloodstream. The room spun in a disorienting haze as he struggled to make sense of the whirlwind of chaos. The taste of suspicion lingered on his tongue as he pondered the identity of his attacker.

Thoughts of Rachel Jillian, the enigmatic woman who had entered his life like a tempest, flooded his mind. Her name whispered through his thoughts, etching itself into his memory. The memory of their first encounter emerged like a phantom, the pulsating lights of the club flickering in his mind's eye. The thumping beats resonated within him, intertwining with their conversation like a rhythmic dance.

Bancroft couldn't say why and how she suddenly filled his head, nor could he wipe it off.

The scent of perfumed desire mingled with the electric energy that crackled between them. It was as if the air had become charged with an intoxicating magnetism. The taste of her laughter, sweet and alluring, danced upon his senses, mingling with the lingering saltiness of the sea that forever clung to his skin.

But beneath the surface of their passionate bond, Bancroft seemed to believe that there had always been a lingering shadow, a whispered warning that he had chosen to ignore. Now, with the taste of violence still fresh upon his lips and deep within the walls of his eyes, he couldn't help but suspect that Rachel's presence in his life had unleashed a malevolent force that sought to tear them apart.

Are they after her or him?

Drawing in a steadying breath, Bancroft summoned his resolve. The room fell into an eerie silence, the weight of the unspoken hanging heavy in the air. He knew he had to confront Rachel as logically as he could to delve deeper into the depths of whatever threat she held. The scent of danger hung like a fog, its tendrils reaching out to grip his soul, beckoning him into the depths of the mystery.

As dawn began to break, casting a soft golden glow across the room, Bancroft emerged from the remnants of the night's chaos. His body ached from the violent encounter, bruises forming like dark blooms across his skin. The grip of the pepper spray on his face had long licensed, leaving just a fragment he barely felt. He stood tall, his senses sharpened, ready to face the shadows on his path.

The room, once a sanctuary, had become a battlefield—a canvas splattered with the remnants of his fight for survival. He surveyed the shattered glass scattered across the floor, the twisted remnants of his assailant's intrusion. Each shard glimmered with a malevolent beauty, reflecting fractured fragments of a world turned upside down.

What is happening? He hushed. Burglary in Capeton was an everyday scenario as reported by the pot-bellied cops from the Capeton Police Department. Attacks like the one he witnessed rarely made it to the PD's records. They happen once in a blue moon, except the victims keep it to themselves.

Bancroft's gaze drifted to the window, now an open portal to the outside world. It was through this shattered barrier that his assailant had escaped, disappearing into the cloak of night. The night, a witness to his struggle, held its secrets close, whispering tales of darkness and danger.

He draped his hand on the rim of the window glass, studying it in grave detail as he scouted for clues. Even a drop of bloodstain on the glass was enough to uncover who was behind the gutful mask. The Forensic department would opt for his hair without blood, and Bancroft was too soaked in thought for such a search.

His mind spun with questions, thoughts intertwining like tangled vines. Who could orchestrate such an attack? Why had they targeted him? And most unsettling of all, how did Rachel fit into this sinister puzzle? Memories of their first meeting flooded his consciousness, their initial encounter a captivating dance of fate and desire.

The club, a den of pulsating energy, had brought them together. It was where he'd touch down occasionally when the weight of nothingness hit hard on him. The scent of spilt drinks and ' the rhythmic thump of music had enveloped them, creating a backdrop against which their connection blossomed. Their eyes had locked, a magnetic pull drawing them closer, sparking a conversation that flowed effortlessly.

"Mind if I join you" Bancroft had asked, his voice a low, gravelly whisper.

Rachel had looked up, a mischievous glint in her eyes, her lips curving into a smile."I was hoping you'd ask."

Bancroft had lagged his head backwards and pulled a smile."You caught my eyes. Huh", he mumbled, drifting his barstool closer.

She jerked into a smiling fit that exposed her even snow-white teeth."I thought you'd knock your glass off" She paused and stroked her ginger-brown hair to the side."In admiration of a beauty that glows even in the dark."

Bancroft had gulped his glass, nodded behind them where the rest of the alcohol-driven partygoers were dancing and stretched his hand forward.
"Let's dance."

Their lives had become entangled from that moment, a whirlwind of stolen glances, shared laughter and whispered secrets. Their dialogues echoed through Bancroft's mind like a symphony, the powerful verbs of their words entwined in a web of intimacy.
But even amidst the intoxicating whirlwind of their connection, there had always been a shadow lingering at the edge. Bancroft had always felt that lowly itch but couldn't find enough reason to go a-digging. He could no longer ignore the tendrils of doubt that snaked through his consciousness. Rachel's past remained a mystery, her secrets like uncharted territory within the depths of his heart. It fell on him clearly that he barely knew her and should do better.

As he sat on the edge of the bed, bruises blooming like dark constellations on his skin, Bancroft pieced together the fragments of his thoughts. The realization settled in his mind like shards of broken glass littered on the floor of his room—the attack was not a random act of violence. It was a direct hit, not even a miss target.

A mixture of determination and fear coursed through his veins. He couldn't allow himself to become a pawn in a twisted game of deceit—especially not when he didn't know it existed. With every fibre of his being, Bancroft knew he had to confront Rachel in whatever way he could to peel back the layers of her past. Hopefully, that's the only way to unearth the truth hidden beneath.

As the first rays of sunlight filtered through the window, casting a warm glow upon the room, Bancroft steeled himself for the coming battles. The deed had been done—he had been ushered in the light of a dark circle he never knew existed in Capeton. With his heightened senses and resolve unyielding, Bancroft felt that he might soon get on a journey that would test his mettle and push him to the limits of his strength.

But he had to start from somewhere from the crime scene where it all began. He jerked off the bed when the doorbell went. His eyes darted to the wall clock— *7:02 am.*

The cops were at the door!

CHAPTER TWO

LIKE TUMOR, SUSPICIONS grow. They don't blow through one's mind overnight like hurricanes. In flickers, Bancroft began to coalesce the tiny and fit the puzzles together. He couldn't say how, but he smelt a foul play—oozing right out of Rachel's direction. He couldn't stop thinking about it, not when remnants of whiskey and cognacs influenced the circumstances surrounding their first meeting.

He loved her, no doubt. The realization made him ponder what he might have ignored to have her all to himself.

First off.

No sane man dates striper, he thought!

The neon lights flickered and pulsed synchronously, with the thumping bass reverberating through the crowded club. Smoke machines cast an ethereal haze that hung in the air, blending with the energy of the pulsating crowd. As Bancroft stepped into the club, the sensory turf whacked his senses—flashes of colourful lights, the smell of sweat mingled with the sweet scent of alcohol, and the reverberating beat that seemed to penetrate deep into his bones. He wasn't new to club life but had a better reason for showing up that night. Nothing else mattered more than that.

The club was a haven for the night creatures, a gathering place for those seeking refuge from the monotony of everyday life. Bodies moved synchronously on the dance floor, and their movements were fluid and uninhibited, a collective expression of freedom and desire.

The air was thick with anticipation, an electric current that crackled through the space, infusing the atmosphere with an intoxicating energy.

Bancroft's eyes darted through the crowd, searching for Rachel amidst the pulsating sea of bodies. That was what brought him there. And that was the only place she could be found. Strippers don't miss the party, no matter whose ox is gored.

She could always be seen there!

After a few more minutes of tearing through the gyrating crowd, Bancroft sighted her from a distance. Her presence had always been a comfort and a source of intrigue, but tonight, something felt different. He noticed a subtle change in her demeanour, a guardedness that had not been there before. It gnawed at his instincts, fueling a sense of unease that tightened his chest.

As he walked through the throng of dancers, a tall figure bumped into him, spilling a crimson-hued cocktail onto his pristine white shirt.

Shit! You son of a bitch!

The red liquor cascaded down Bancroft's Shirt, forming a red hue stretching from his chest to his lower left ribs. Irritation flickered across Bancroft's face as the man murmured and dashed into the crowd.

Bancroft felt humiliated. But even that didn't matter. Getting to Rachel did.

Swiftly, he clenched his fists, feeling the dampness seep through his fingertips, the coldness of the drink a stark contrast to the heat of the club. His eyes rifled right towards the spot he saw Rachel. He launched closer and then let out frustrating bloat. She wasn't the one.

Someone looked like her.

Bancroft mumbled a *sorry* and waltzed aside after swinging the lady around, thinking she was Rachel.

He had to try harder. He had no other way. After she confirmed that he could catch up with her in a *Boogie Down,* her phone line went utterly unreachable.

Slowly but steadily, he shuffled ahead. She certainly might be stuck somewhere!

The club's interior was always a visual feast—a wheel of colours and textures that assaulted the senses. The walls were adorned with graffiti, vibrant hues splashed across a backdrop of urban decay. Mismatched chairs and tables were scattered, their surfaces marred with countless rings from spilt drinks and flickering candle flames.

These little details made *Boogie Down* some sensation in Capeton —even stretching as far as Montebello.

The Turkish brothers who run the club call it *Boogie Down,* but even the least excited clubber won't be patient enough to add to the name. They all knew it as *Boogie* — the best club in Capeton. The only place you'll find the most essential elements of Capeton street life under one roof.

Best women.

Craziest ballers.

Big spenders.

The big barons too!

The music swelled, reaching a crescendo as the DJ expertly blended beats, his hands dancing across the decks with skilful precision. The melodies pulsated through the club, absorbing the laughter, the conversations, and the occasional shouts. It was a symphony of chaos, a hypnotic rhythm that invited patrons to lose themselves in the moment.

It was hard and hot, but Bancroft had to reject all that fun.

Not tonight!

As Bancroft moved further into the club's heart, he caught glimpses of seductive performances on elevated stages. Dancers, adorned in sequined costumes, moved with sensual grace, their bodies twisting and contorting to the rhythm of the music. The scent of sweat mixed with the intoxicating perfume of the performers created an intoxicating blend that filled the air.

But amid the captivating spectacle, Bancroft couldn't shake off the feeling that something was amiss. He had expected to find Rachel here, but she was nowhere to be seen. He had never gone that deep into *Boogie* without sighting Rachel.

Anxiety tightened its grip around his heart, constricting his breath as he anxiously scanned the crowd. Questions and doubts plagued his mind — had she deliberately lied about her whereabouts?

The club's atmosphere, once exhilarating, now seemed suffocating. The pounding music became a relentless assault on Bancroft's ears, the lights blinding and disorienting. Sweat trickled down his forehead, mingling with the remnants of the spilt drink, and he wiped it away with an agitated swipe of his hand.

Just as Bancroft was about to abandon his search and succumb to the suffocating disappointment, a glimmer of hope sparked within him. He caught a fleeting glimpse of Rachel's ginger-brown hair, wrapped in a ponytail just as she liked it, as she disappeared into the dense crowd.

That must be her. He was sure this time around.

Shards of excitement surged through his veins, propelling him forward, weaving between bodies, and pushing through the pulsating mass of people. He couldn't afford to miss her.

Not again!

Some drunk dancers cursed and kicked as he staggered past them in desperation. He wasn't as fast as he wished, but he wasn't too slow. He saw Rachel as she halted before a hefty bearded black-suited man.

But as he reached the spot where he had seen her, she vanished like a phantom, leaving a space and a deepening sense of betrayal. The man who stood with her had equally disappeared. The music drowned out his frustrated sigh, swallowed by the cacophony of the club.

Bancroft felt anger and confusion wash over him, his mind swirling with unanswered questions. The stain on his shirt was a stark reminder of the chaos that had unfolded within and beyond the club's confines. His instincts screamed at him to uncover the truth and delve deeper into Rachel's hidden past and the mysteries surrounding her. At that juncture, he had just one thought.

Is she safe?

With a heavy heart and a frown, Bancroft turned his back on the pulsating club, leaving behind the suffocating atmosphere and the shattered fragments of his trust. The journey to uncover the truth had only begun, and he was prepared to navigate the depths of Rachel's secrets, no matter the cost.

He had no idea what she was hiding, but he had never been so sure about something as he was sure about his instincts towards Rachel — his stripper girlfriend.

Where is she?

CHAPTER THREE

THE NIGHT DRAPED THE ROOM in an inky blackness, broken only by the faint glow of moonlight filtering through the curtains. The lights were out, and Rachel didn't sleep with the lights on, which became a rule Bancroft learned to adapt to.

On the king-size bed, they two lay, entwined in each other's embrace, their bodies nestled beneath the soft sheets. The hush of their breathing filled the room, becoming the loudest silence therein.

She had phoned him later after his fruitless search at *Boogie*. She had briefly gone to see her boss in his office and didn't notice she had a dead battery. The peace offer was to spend the night with him. Always, it went crazy and good until sleep swept them off their feet.

Suddenly, a sharp creak reverberated through the silence, sending a shiver down Bancroft's spine. Awake, his senses heightened, and he jerked his frame off the bed, his muscles tensing instantly. A cold wave of dread washed over him as his eyes adjusted to the darkness, searching for the source of the disturbance.

In the shadows stood a figure, masked and foreboding, his presence an ominous spectre in the room. Adrenaline sped through Bancroft's veins as he sprang into action. He reached for the silver pistol beneath the pillow, its weight a reassuring presence in his grip.

He had yet another company.

As if on the initial thrust of a ballistic missile, the figure lunged forward ruthlessly, a blur of malevolence in the night. Bancroft twisted and rolled, narrowly evading the first strike. A symphony of chaos erupted, and the room became a battlefield as the struggle ensued.

More intense than it was at the first encounter, fists collided with bone, the sickening thuds muffled by the moment's intensity. Each blow was met with a counterattack, the dance of violence punctuated by gasps and grunts. Perhaps, the figure had learned from the last bout and not even Bancroft remained untaught. Bancroft's senses heightened, his focus narrowing to the singular objective of protecting himself and Rachel.

The room became a battleground of desperation and survival. The scent of sweat permeated the air, mingling with the metallic tang of blood. Bancroft was bleeding, and his upper lid took on a new shape as the knock from the figure landed on it. Shadows danced upon the walls, elongated and distorted by the flickering moonlight, mirroring the ebb and flow of the fierce struggle.

Bancroft's heart pounded in his chest, the rhythm echoing like a war drum, reverberating through his veins as adrenaline gathered. The unrelenting figure, a shadow of fury, pressed forward with relentless energy, his charge slightly matching Bancroft's resilience. Every step his assailant took seemed to be fueled by a dark determination, each movement calculated to inflict maximum damage.

A surge of pain shot through Bancroft's body as a blow landed, a thunderous impact that momentarily blurred his vision. The world spun around him as he fought to regain focus, his senses honed to the chaos unfolding before him. Blood trickled from a split lip, mingling with the sweat that streamed down his face, but he refused to yield, his resolve unwavering.

It was a hit for a hit—an intricate dance of pain and retaliation.

Bancroft countered swiftly, delivering blows that echoed with his fury burning. His fists collided with flesh, the impact resonating through the room like thunderclaps, momentarily drowning out Rachel's fearful cries.

Tired from the violent chaos, Rachel clung to the bed sheets, her eyes wide with fear and worry across her face. Her voice, laden with urgency, cut through the tumultuous air, urging Bancroft to be cautious. "Bancroft, be careful!" she cried, her words a lifeline, a surge of protectiveness welling within him, giving him renewed strength.

Minutes stretched into an eternity, time-warped by the intensity of the struggle. The room became a battleground. Furniture toppled and shattered objects scattered across the floor. Bancroft moved with the agility of a predator, his training guiding him through the darkness, his instincts sharpened by years of honing his skills.

Yet, he couldn't help but admit one thing; the figure must be some hardened serial killer. He at no point came off as one who left things to chance. His moves are sleek and targeted. His hits are sharp and sturdy. His break-ins are unbelievably stealthy — second to none Bancroft had ever seen.

Each punch thrown was a calculated risk, every block a desperate attempt to fend off the relentless assault. Bancroft fought to defend himself and protect the one he loved, his every action fueled by a resolute fate. Sweat-soaked and battered, he pushed through the pain, the echoes of his heartbeat drowning out the chaos surrounding him.

He'd have ended the whole drama long ago, but his gun had been knocked out in the initial onslaught. It lay just out of reach, a cruel reminder of his vulnerability in this desperate struggle. The room seemed to close in on him, its walls closing like the jaws of a relentless beast. The figure came back overly prepared.

And then, during the chaos, a gunshot cracked through the room, its sound cutting through the air like a lightning bolt. It flung the room into commotion.

For a brief moment, time stood still as smoke spiralled from the barrel, the figure frozen in his tracks. Bancroft's eyes widened as he registered the sight before him, the mysterious figure standing motionless, a mask of shock and pain etched onto his masked face.

But as quickly as the gunshot had shattered the room's deafening symphony, the figure seized the opportunity, his instincts as sharp as Bancroft'. In a swift motion, he darted towards the window, his hand skillfully unlatching it without breaking the glass. With a final glance back at Bancroft, a mix of fury and frustration etched on his features as he vanished into the night, again swallowed by the darkness from which he emerged.

The room fell silent, save for the echoes of their struggle that hung heavily in the air. Bancroft stood, his body bruised, his chest heaving with exhaustion and adrenaline. Sweat mingled with blood dripping from his brow as he surveyed the remnants of the battle around him.

Rachel rushed to his side, trembling hands reaching to caress his face." Are you okay" she whispered, her voice filled with relief and concern. Bancroft nodded slowly, his gaze still fixed on the empty window, the weight of what had just transpired settling upon him.

They were safe, for now, but the threat loomed, a presence that lingered in the shadows, waiting for its next opportunity to strike. Bancroft knew that this was far from over, that the fight had only begun.

As he turned away from the shattered remnants of their sanctuary, his resolve burned brighter than ever, fueling his resolve to protect Rachel and end the relentless attacker who haunted their lives.

Now, he was sure of one thing; Rachel was clean. But then, another question reached the core of his worries.

Who's after me?

In the aftermath of the chaotic struggle, the room lay in ruins, a testament to the attack that almost disappeared with Bancroft's life. Bancroft stood amidst the debris, his gaze sweeping over the wreckage, each broken fragment echoing the pain and turmoil that had engulfed him while lost in the centre of all that mess. His mind raced, searching for answers amidst the chaos, for the identity and motives of the assailants who had unleashed this nightmarish ordeal.

Like in the previous attack, he stepped aside, watching the men from the forensic unit of Capeton Police Department doing their jobs. Nothing substantial came off the scene inspection of the previous attack and Bancroft was slightly sure that the story won't be any different from what it had always been.

As the weight of the situation threatened to crush him, a familiar voice cut through the haze."Bancroft", a deep baritone resonated, filled with concern and hastiness. It was Homicide Detective Christopher Hunter, a trusted friend and former comrade-in-arms. They had joined the Capeton Police Department together after leaving the Navy, forging an unbreakable bond.

But Bancroft left the Police. He loved the job and the peace that comes with solving crimes and putting smiles on people's faces but for more than two decades, he had trailed the path of crime-fighting; from the Navy to the Police, without ever coming to an admittance if that's what he truly wanted for his life. When he felt the need to take an uncommon step, he did. He seemed fit to sit back and staff his growing businesses in Capeton and Montebello before looking out for what fate would morph him into.

Hunter never left. He was made for the guns. They both knew that!

Hunter's sharp eyes took in the devastation, his gaze unwavering."What the hell happened here" he demanded, his voice tinged with urgency.

Bancroft turned to face Hunter, his expression a mixture of exhaustion and grim resolve."He came back," Bancroft retorted.
Hunter shuffled further into the room, his piercing eyes raiding the ruins as the forensic men gathered the fragments into nylon specimen bags and labelled them.
"This morning," Hunter asked.
"Last night", Rachel chipped in, her voice sober and dull.

Detective Hunter nodded and moved towards the window, maintaining a distance between him and the forensic men. He was the boss. It was his crime scene but he feared contaminating it. He couldn't afford to miss any chances.

"You're sure it's him," Detective Hunter asked almost without looking at Bancroft.

"Twice, Hunter. I've wrestled that son of a bitch twice. The energy only grew wilder. The moves never changed" Bancroft explained, his head in his palms.

He continued."It was a relentless attack, Chris," he replied, his voice heavy with the weight of the memories of the attacks."At the slightest chance, he comes out of nowhere, driven by some strange motive."

Hunter's gaze hardened, his jaw clenching."Strange motive"

"I can't say if he's out to kill or just maim."

"You wouldn't let that happen, would you" The detective chipped in.

"But he had his chances. He had many more chances to pull the trigger or a knife than I had in whacking him down and ripping off the mask on his face."

"We won't let him get away with this, Bancroft," he declared, his voice filled with conviction.

"I'll find him."

Their eyes locked an unspoken understanding passing between them. Hunter was a detective and a steadfast ally in this personal war. An attack on Bancroft was an attack on him—he was all out to pin down whoever was behind that mask.

Even up till the evening of the same day, Bancroft and Rachel stood on the sidelines, their faces etched with weariness and anxiety as they awaited at least a hint that'd shed light on the attacker's identity. Bancroft didn't care about his motive. At that point, his identity mattered more than anything else. When he's known, he can't hide. Even if he lives in Montebello or its outskirts, Bancroft and Hunter will find him.

Bancroft's phone's steady but low ring stabbed the silent suspense between Bancroft and Rachel. She was lost in the bathroom, perhaps, curled into the bathtub, when the call came.

Bancroft recognized the voice at the expense of one statement."I've got something for you."

It's Detective Hunter.

After the lengthy tests were concluded, he got good news from the Forensic team.

"You were right. It's the same asshole. Fabric patterns from the first attack matched with those from the last even though this holds no clue about his identity," Detective Hunter explained subtly.

"Nothing's tangible yet."

"I wonder how hard you had hit him. He left bloodstains on your drawers this time."

"That's enough clues, Hunter."

There came a brief silence before Detective Hunter continued."He's no longer off the radar. Our results came out positive. But, it's pretty unclear."

"Who is he."

"Otis Crane", Detective Hunter announced."Does that ring a bell"

Bancroft thought for a few seconds before his admittance."I probably met lots of Otis but not a Crane. What have you got."

"54. Lumberman at Dream Farms. No criminal record. Lives on Clifford Boulevard"

"You've got to be kidding me! A fifty-year-old can't kick my ass, Hunter. Am I that weak"

"I analyzed that more than you just did, Bancroft. But there's something you failed to mention."

A cold aura swept through Bancroft when Detective Hunter's words sunk through him. He couldn't readily think of any obvious detail he missed in his narration of the two encounters with the so-called Otis Crane.

"What are you talking about," he asked. "Hugs Cafe. 6:00 pm. Don't be late."

Bancroft and Detective Christopher Hunter found Otis's residence—a rundown, weathered house tucked away in a forgotten corner in Clifford Boulevard—a suburb of Capeton that was once a military zone during the civil unrest that stretched from Montebello through Capeton and beyond.

Otis' apartment exuded an air of desolation, reflecting its owner's seemingly forgotten existence. Bancroft and Hunter approached cautiously, their steps measured, each heartbeat resonating with the moment's weight. On his end, Bancroft felt guilty for underrating Otis. Detective Hunter told him back at the car.

You rate him so lowly, friend.

A shiver ran down Bancroft's spine as they knocked on the door. The door creaked open, revealing a dishevelled man, his eyes filled with shadows. Otis Crane—a figure marred by hardship and obscured by mystery. He gazed at them with a mix of defiance and resignation.

To Bancroft, he was nothing to be compared to the figure he wrestled with on two occasions.

Detective Hunter flashed his ID," Detective Christopher Hunter. Capeton Police Department"

Bancroft stepped forward, his tone straight and plain." Otis Crane, we need answers," he declared, his words echoing through the stillness of the dilapidated house.

Otis's eyes bore into Bancroft, flickering with a storm of emotions. He then swung his stare in Detective Hunter's direction."Answers to what."

Detective Hunter heaved a sigh and signalled Bancroft to hold back a bit."Heard of the attacks in Brooklyn."

"None that I can remember", Otis interjected sharply.

"A couple had a murder attempt twice in a week and."

"Is that supposed to be the reason you're interrogating me"

Otis wasn't cooperating. He didn't even show a sigh that he'd cooperate anytime soon. Bancroft was losing it. He hated himself for not having latched him a punch to his prominent nose when he first showed his disproportionately ageing face.

Detective Hunter slammed the file in his hands on Otis's chest, stepping aside."The DNA found at the crime scene belongs to only two persons. The attack victim and some Otis Crane, a lumberman in Dream Farms who lives in some ridiculous cubicle in the much dreaded Clifford Boulevard. Does that ring a bell"

Silence hung over the three men as Otis studied the pictures he retrieved from the file Detective Hunter gave him. The brief silence gave Bancroft ample time to raid the sitting room with the eyes of an eagle.

"I have no idea what you're talking about", Otis announced, dropping the file on the table that separates him from Detective Hunter.

"You know these forensic procedures do not lie. Right," Bancroft chimed in, waltzing closer.

"I am not too dumb not to understand that. But that will never make me accept what's not right. I have no idea what you want. I know no couple who got attacked. I know no one who could attack anyone. You're in the wrong apartment."

"I need answers, Otis", Bancroft stressed, closing in on Otis, who had long grown used to their presence.

Detective Hunter wondered what Otis was about to say. The older man didn't get to say it. Bancroft's hard punch sent him to the ground in a split second.

"You have no idea what pain you've caused me. And. I. Will. Put. A. Bullet. In. Your. Head. If. Lie. To. Me. Again" Bancroft barked. Detective Hunter held him back as Otis struggled to get back on his feet.

Otis staggered upward, laughing instead of cursing and crying."You think you're entitled to answers. Huh", he retorted, his voice laced with bitterness."You have no idea what's coming for you."

Bancroft, taken aback, exchanged a glance with Detective Hunter."What do you mean" he pressed, his voice steady but tinged with urgency.

Otis's gaze hardened, his voice dripping with accusation."What I mean is what we both know", he nodded to Bancroft and then turned to Detective Hunter" And they do not."

Confusion crept into Bancroft's mind, leaving his eyes dilated. Again, he knocked down Otis. This time, with a kick that found its way to the man's midsection.

Even in sheer pain, Otis grumbled and said things that got Bancroft and Detective Hunter lost and confused."You destroyed everything, Bancroft", he hissed."Your actions in the past unleashed a chain of events that led us all down this path."

Bancroft's mind whirled, memories flashing before his eyes."I don't understand", he whispered, his voice a fragile thread.

Otis's eyes gleamed with anger and pain."You left us behind", he spat, the words laced with venomous intensity."You turned your back on the ones who fought alongside you while we paid the price."

He left us. Who? Paid the price. What price? Questions brimmed Bancroft's head. He felt an itch to pelt Otis with blows but at the same time, he needed him to keep talking. Not to triple his confusion but at least to see if he'd end up saying something more reasonable.

Hunter stepped forward, his voice calm but commanding."Otis, we want to make this right", he interjected, his words laced with empathy."We want to understand and help."

Bancroft didn't love the sound of that. Even at the Capeton Police Department, that was his chief turn-off about Detective Hunter's approach to policing. The former Navy SEAL was always ready for negotiations with people he was supposed to knock down and put cuffs around their wrists and ankles.

Otis's face contorted with bitter anguish."You can't undo what's been done", he seethed."The scars run deep, and the only justice left is the one we seek ourselves."

As the tension in the room mounted, a chilling silence fell, broken only by the echoes of their strained breaths. The weight of the past seemed to suffocate the present as if an inescapable destiny entwined their lives.

At that moment, a gunshot cracked through the air, shattering the fragile air of peace. The room erupted into chaos as Otis, fueled by a desperate determination, seized the opportunity to escape. He sprinted toward the window, flinging it open with a fierce resolve. Bancroft and Hunter lunged forward, their hands outstretched, but it was too late.

Otis sped into the garden and then out to the streets through the garage, leaving behind a trail of questions and shattered hope. Bancroft and Hunter stood, their chests heaving, their eyes locked on the empty window.

"He wants something from you, Bancroft," Hunter whispered, his voice laden with desperation and concern."And until we know what he wants, he'll remain a ghost in your life — our lives. "

Bancroft nodded, his jaw clenched in disbelief. The path ahead seemed darker than he had ever imagined. Alas, his fears came alive when Detective Hunter stopped at the doorpost and turned to him. "What do you know that we do not."

The question droned the room, sinking deep into Bancroft's Subconscious. He was about to answer it when he felt fierce taps on his arms.
"I have to go now! It's past 7 am."
It's Rachel. It was morning. She was about to leave for one of her part-time jobs in some bistro at the centre of Capeton.
"Wake up"

CHAPTER FOUR

BANCROFT STOOD OUTSIDE RACHEL'S APARTMENT, the weight of anticipation heavy upon his shoulders. The tip he received had sparked a fire within him—a fire fueled by the need to expose the truth. He knew that within those walls, hidden among the shadows, might lay the key to the past Rachel was hiding so badly.

With a steady hand, he inserted the slim piece of metal into the lock, feeling the tumblers yield to his touch. The click echoed through the hallway, a subtle confirmation that he had breached Rachel's fortress. As he stepped inside, the door closing silently behind him, the air thickened with palpable tension.

You just broke into your lover's apartment.

His heart kept ringing that statement in his head.

The apartment lay shrouded in darkness, and it was lifeless and still. The silence whispered secrets, and Bancroft moved cautiously, his senses alive to every sound and subtle shift in the atmosphere. He scanned the room, his gaze fixated on every nook and cranny, searching for any sign leading him closer to the truth.

He put on the lighting. He needed it.

His footsteps, muffled by the plush carpet, carried him toward a locked drawer beneath a mundane stack of paperwork. It called to him, its contents begging to be unearthed. His instincts didn't move an inch away from it. It dwelled there. His brows contorted as he retrieved his lock-picking tools and knelt in front of the drawer.

Bancroft's hands moved with practised precision, expertly manipulating the seemingly tough lock of the drawer. Each click, each subtle shift of the pins, brought him closer to uncovering and breaking into the meat of whatever was inside the drawer. His heart thudded in his chest, the adrenaline coursing through his veins as the drawer yielded to his skilled touch.

As the drawer slid open, suspense coursed through his veins. It revealed a secret archive, a treasure trove of documents, photographs, and files that could be fragments of the truth he was looking for — even though he had no idea what it was.

On every move of his hand, the room seemed to hum with the weight of the revelations yet to be unveiled.

His eyes darted from one file to another, each a potential piece of the puzzle he was determined to solve. With trembling hands, he delved into the depth of the heap of files, immersing himself in anything he could get his hands on.

He saw photographs that depicted Rachel in different guises, her eyes reflecting many. He at first understood that those could be pictures of her younger self he never got to see. He dug, fighting to find something tangible in what suddenly became information chaos. Alas, one item caught his attention — a passport.

The Spanish passport bore the name"Jennifer Alvarez" and its pages contained the key to Rachel's true identity. As Bancroft held it in his hands, he felt a mixture of triumph and frustration. It was a monumental discovery, an undeniable truth that Rachel was living a life of deception. But he knew that the passport alone wouldn't reveal the full extent of her secrets. Is she Spanish? What could she be doing with a Spanish passport?

His heart raced, yearning for more answers, more clues to complete the puzzle. With the drastically dimming hope he had left, he continued to search, scouring every corner of the apartment for additional evidence. Drawers were opened, closets examined, and furniture turned over, but the apartment seemed to hold its secrets tightly.

That was all!

The intensity of the search consumed Bancroft, his mind consumed by the need to expose the truth. He rifled through files, peered at photographs, and scrutinized every piece of evidence. Each discovery, no matter how small, seemed to heighten his anticipation.

After both were attacked, he thought his suspicions about Rachel had died. But it resurrected. As the investigation took awry turns, he felt Rachel was hiding more. But he just couldn't say what it was.

But as the minutes turned into hours, frustration began to gnaw at him. The apartment remained silent as if mocking his relentless pursuit. Bancroft felt a sinking feeling in his chest, realizing that the answers he sought might elude him for now.

Exhausted, he reluctantly closed the last drawer, accepting that he had reached a dead end. The Spanish passport, however, remained clutched tightly in his hand, a constant reminder of the mysteries that still lay unresolved.

Bancroft stepped back, his gaze lingering on Rachel's apartment one last time. He knew he had to regroup, reassess his approach, and dig deeper into Rachel's tangled web of deception.

With a heavy sigh, Bancroft turned away, the weight of the unknown resting heavily on his shoulders. The road ahead was fraught with dangers and uncertainties, but he was willing to navigate its treacherous twists and turns.

However, he almost jumped out of his skin when footsteps came loud in the hallway. There's someone at the door.

Shit!

Bancroft silently followed a certain woman through the crowded club, and his eyes trained on her every move. His instincts told him she was up to something and he saw it. He was at the club to find Rachel but as he observed the woman who moved too sleek for somebody with a shape such as hers, he noticed a sense of purpose in her steps, a determination etched across her face.

Bancroft saw it. The woman was slowly following Rachel. It occurred to him that she could be a dead danger when she murmured after putting her fingers into her left ear. She was communicating. With who? Bancroft spun around, observing if he's been watched too. He saw no sign.

His gaze focused on the woman as she entered the dimly lit restroom. The pulsating music masked the sound of their footsteps as Bancroft followed her in, the anticipation building within him. He had to confront her and discover why she was spying on Rachel.

Inside the confined space of the restroom, the air became charged with electric energy. Bancroft's heart pounded in his chest as he positioned himself strategically, ready to confront her. He had to tread carefully, for he knew not the full extent of her intentions.

The woman's blue eyes widened as she caught sight of Bancroft, her expression shifting from surprise to defiance. At that moment, the atmosphere transformed, and the two adversaries prepared to engage in a battle that would lay bare the secrets they held.

Without uttering a word, Bancroft lunged forward, his movements fluid and calculated. The woman, her training and experience evident, met his attack with equal force. The small restroom became an arena of frenzied movement and clashing bodies.

Their fists connected with a symphony of thuds and grunts, each blow propelled by their relentless staggers. Bancroft fought intensely, fueled by his thirst for answers, while the woman's agility and tenacity countered every strike he delivered.

Their fight was a dance of chaos and skill, a symphony of brute strength and cunning strategy. The confined space offered little room for evasion, forcing them to engage in close combat, where every punch and counterpunch carried the weight of their varying secrets or furies.

Fists meeting flesh echoed through the restroom, mingling with their heavy breathing. Sweat coated their brows, and their bodies were pushed to the brink of exhaustion. But neither was willing to back down. The intensity of their fight mirrored the depths of their conviction.

With a swift move to the left, Bancroft dodged her punch and grabbed her from the side, pulling her up and high enough to smash her against the rack stand that housed the towels in the restroom. On the ground, she volleyed her left leg right into Bancroft's ill-positioned thigh, which he reeled sideward.

They both made fresh moves but this time, with guns. She pointed hers to Bancroft's forehead while he pointed his to the side of her head, just above her left ear.

Breathing heavily, Bancroft's voice rasped with exertion."Whom are you working for."

The woman's features softened, her gaze no longer filled with hostility but tinged with newfound respect. She reached under her black leather jacket and shoved her badge towards Bancroft.

"Detective Elaine Murphy, Montebello PD"

Bancroft's hands weakened as he dog-trotted backwards and leaned against the sink behind him.

"What do you want," Bancroft asked.

"I've been tracking a Spanish refugee", Elaine replied.

"Beyond your jurisdiction."

She smiled. One that held flickers of pain from the many hits and punches she received."Don't you think these limits do not count when a high-profile criminal is on the loose"

"Who is he," Bancroft asked.

"Who"

"Your suspect"

Elaine chuckled. This time, she was on her feet. The gurgling of water engulfed the restroom as she watched the blood off her blonde face."Our suspect, you mean, Bancroft Logan."

Bancroft was up and surprised. He sheathed his gun into his waist and reached for the tap.

"Are you one of those psychos deployed as undercovers?" he asked.

"Whatever you wish to see me as"

"I'm surprised you know me. Should I"

"I mean, we all know ourselves if we wanna be honest to each other."

That was the word that fit Bancroft turning towards her again. He indeed didn't know her.

"You know me too well," he asked.

"Not like your biographer does but yes. Former Navy SEAL. Lieutenant Junior Grade. Gave up the military dream after a heavy defeat in Havana."

"That's enough" Bancroft pushed her in. He felt she had proved her point and needed to go straight to why she came hunting a suspect as far as Capeton.

"Who are you looking for."

"Jennifer Alvarez"

The name got to Bancroft like an electric shock. He didn't have to think twice to remember that that was the same name on the passport he stole from Rachel's apartment. Again, Bancroft will dash towards Elaine, grabbing her fiercely and slamming her against the wall. She didn't fight back. She only struggled to breathe.

"Who the hell are you? Why are you after Rachel? I saw you spying on her," he growled and slit his finger into her ears but found nothing. He had seen her fiddling with something in her ears. However, even though she wore something, she might have lost it during their fight.

"She's Jennifer Alvarez. But you know her as Rachel Jillian. That's what everyone around her knows her as" Elaine began to explain.

Bancroft was so shocked to keep holding her. He let her go and drifted backwards slowly until he got back to the sink.

"Who the hell is she? "Nothing to worry too much about, at least now. Spanish refugee. Lawyer by profession. Should be 23 in a month or two."

All of that was too far from all Bancroft knew about Rachel. He knew her as a twenty-three-year-old who never had a degree and might get one. The revelations left him bare and numb.

"I know. These are top secrets."

"How do you know them."

"Four good years. For four years, I've been on her tracks. I know more than you do, but there's more we both do not know and should fight to know before it gets too late."

"What do you know," Bancroft asked, assuming a tone subtler than any he had ever used since they two began talking.

"Rachel is part of an ongoing investigation that has cut across counties and towns. It all began in Montebello. A bigger conspiracy is at play, one involving dangerous forces."

"Spy, you mean."

"Rachel is deadlier than we can imagine."

Bancroft's mind raced as he absorbed Elaine's words, his initial suspicion giving way to a flicker of understanding. He had been unaware of the vastness of the conspiracy surrounding Rachel, and now, faced with this revelation, he knew they had a common goal.

Bancroft lowered his guard, reluctantly recognizing that Elaine was not his enemy but a potential ally. The fight had been a crucible, forging a bond of shared purpose.

"What's your plan" Bancroft caught himself asking.

"Get to her before they do", Elaine responded.

"They? Who"

"The attackers"

CHAPTER FIVE

" WHERE WAS YOUR FATHER LAST NIGHT"

Detective Christopher Hunter's voice cut through the tension-filled room, his tone laced with urgency and suspicion. The question hung in the air, its weight bearing on them all.

Daniel is the seventeen-year-old son of Otis Crane, the chief suspect in Bancroft's attacks. He was the only one at home when they touched down at the apartment.

Daniel stood before Hunter and Bancroft, slightly uneasy, his eyes darting nervously between the two detectives. The room seemed to hold its breath, waiting for Daniel's response, for the truth that would shape their next steps.

Hunter's piercing gaze bore into Daniel's like he was trying to read the unspoken words in his mind through his eyes. He needed to ascertain the authenticity of Daniel's words to determine if they could rely on the alibi he'd be presenting.

Did he know they'll be coming? Has his father told him anything?

Detective Hunter observed the scene, his mind buzzing with curiosity and suspicion. Daniel's presence in the room intrigued him, for it indicated a potential connection to the ongoing investigation—having the son of a chief suspect who's old enough to talk came off as a colossal flex, despite coming with some slight ethical barriers. He understood the weight of this moment, the significance of the answers they sought.

Detective Hunter asked again, this time slow and gentle."Where was your father last night."

Daniel swallowed hard, his voice quivering with anxiety and fear."He was... He was with us, at home," Daniel stammered, his words coming out in fragments. His youthful face betrayed a hint of desperation, as if he too sought to unravel the mysteries that had consumed their lives.
"You wanna share why that took you forever to respond," Detective Hunter asked, gawking at his face, straight into his jittering eyeballs. "I-I-I don't know. I'm not hiding anything," Daniel explained.

"I didn't say you are. Did I" Detective Hunter retorted.

"You sound like you do", Daniel mumbled, his eyes changing direction. They went for Bancroft who was equally staring at him intensely.

Detective Hunter leaned forward, his voice steady but demanding."Daniel, you say you all went out as a family last night."

Daniel nodded in response.

"To where"

"To some bistro in Central Capeton."

"The place does have a name. I guess"

"I can't get the name. That was my first time there."

Detective Hunter traded glances with Bancroft and turned to Daniel again."How many of you went there?

"Just the four of us. Me, my Dad and Mom and then my younger sister."

Detective Hunter leaned forward, talking almost in a whisper."Can anyone else prove your father's whereabouts last night?"

Daniel's brows furrowed as he strained to recall the events of the previous evening. The room seemed to hold its breath once more as Daniel's eyes scanned it, searching for a lifeline, a supporting voice to strengthen his claim.

Finally, Daniel's gaze settled on a family photograph adorning the wall. It captured a moment frozen in time, a snapshot of happiness. With a glimmer of hope, he spoke, his voice tinged with a newfound resolve.

"After a burrito at the bistro, my father took us all to a show. It was a special family night out," Daniel explained, his words gaining strength."We were surrounded by people, witnesses who can vouch for us."

"Do we have any in the neighbourhood?" Detective Hunter asked.

"About three. Mr Rupert lives two apartments away. Ms Lowpole lives at the house at the edge of the street while old lady Tina lives opposite us. They all saw us last night."

Hunter's stern expression softened ever so slightly, a trace of understanding in his eyes. He knew that the words of a minor needed to be scrutinized, but in this instance, Daniel's account aligned with their initial investigation.

Bancroft rose from his chair, a sense of unease washing over him as he studied the room. It was not the same room he had seen in his dream. There existed a clear-cut difference between the two buildings even though the exact address remained the same. It wasn't as dirty as what he saw in the dream, which wasn't even his primary concern. He felt quizzical about the fact that Otis' record never mentioned that he's got a family.

That'd be the first question he'd ask Detective Hunter when they left the apartment.

As he glanced around, the memories of that intense interrogation resurfaced. He couldn't let go of the things he said. The claims he made and the unexpected escape he pulled.

Hunter's gaze bore into Daniel, his voice laced with determination and compassion."Daniel, we need your cooperation. Your father is a person of interest in an ongoing investigation. We believe he holds crucial information. Are you sure about what you're telling us?"

"I-I just told you all I know."

"When do you all return from the show" Bancroft stepped in.

"Around 7 pm. I can't say the exact minute."

"Where did he go after that," Bancroft asks again.

Daniel's breath hitched, his voice tinged with fear and loyalty. Perhaps, that was a part he never thought of since. "He... he stepped out afterwards."

Bancroft turned to Detective Hunter and then back to Daniel. "Stepped out to where?"

"I don't know. He didn't say anything!" Daniel admitted.

At that point, the conviction was closing in. Why didn't Detective Hunter and Bancroft not go in search of Otis Crane since? The conviction was weak, despite the DNA result. Bancroft made a more significant part of the delay. But, after a woman four apartments away from Bancroft's apartment reported a similar attack to the cops, the need to find Otis became obvious. Even on the third scene of the attack, his DNA was found.

That brought Detective Hunter and Bancroft to his doorpost that Wednesday morning. Now, Daniel was admitting something to what they could bank on.

Hunter's voice softened, a glimmer of understanding breaking through his steely demeanour. "Daniel, we understand that your loyalty lies with your father. But we need the truth, no matter how difficult it may be. It could help us find the person responsible for these attacks."

"Attacks?" Daniel asked with shock ebbed all over his face.

Detective Hunter nodded in response.

"Is that what all of this is about?" Daniel challenged. "You think my father attacked these people?"

The room fell into a heavy silence as Bancroft and Hunter absorbed Daniel's question. They knew they had to feed his ego, no matter how obscure.

"My colleague nor I ever said that. We are carrying out the normal procedure. We ask questions and then build our investigation based on your responses," Detective Hunter explained.

Daniel suddenly wore an ambience of boldness that remained hidden throughout the conversation. "I'm seventeen and I know you're asking me all of these because you think my father either attacked these people or has helped somebody attack them. Isn't that so?"

"It's a normal procedure, Daniel…"

"To my father alone?"

"To everyone we have on our watchlist…"

Detective Hunter chose not to pick an offence. He stepped aside and then turned to the acrylic painting on the sitting room's walls. He shoved his ID into the air as if for Daniel to admire.

"What grade are you, Daniel?" Detective Hunter asked.

"12th," Daniel gruffed.

"You love logic as a topic in Mathematics. Don't you?"

Daniel kept mute. He didn't respond.

"Let's do something quite simple, Daniel. Assume that I'm not a cop. I'm some businessman uptown. If you find my ID card at the murder scene of a loved one, will you come looking for me?"

"I'm not a cop."

"But I believe you'd love to find justice for the people you love and cherish. Don't you?"

Daniel nodded. He was beginning to buy into the narrative.

"The Police can't help. There's no sign of clues. But you have the ID card you saw at the scene before anybody else. Where will your quest for justice begin?"

"Finding the owner of the ID…"

"Why?" Detective Hunter asked amid smiles.

"He might know something that might help."

That was the exact point Detective Hunter wanted to take him to. Bancroft leaned forward and maintained eye contact with Daniel. "We've had three attacks. Your father's DNA was found in all of these three crime scenes. Do you now see why we're looking for him?"

Daniel was left numb and mum. He looked at the two with absolute emptiness in his eyes. He never saw that coming.

Detective Hunter took the lead when he patted Daniel on the shoulder. "Tell him the PD came around!"

Just as they were about to leave the apartment, a shrill ring broke the stillness. The sound cut through the tension, their gazes shifting to Hunter as he answered the call, his face transforming from curiosity to a mask of concern.

Hunter's voice held a tremor of urgency as he spoke into the phone. "I'll be there in 10 minutes?"

There's another attack with two uncommon things. It happened in broad daylight. The victim couldn't make it.

It's officially the attacker's first murder!

The news struck Bancroft like a bolt of lightning, intensifying the gravity of their investigation. Indeed, what lies ahead is quite heavier than what had been seen.

As they exited the apartment, Bancroft's mind whirled with thoughts. The connection between Otis and the attacks remained unclear.

Will he be affiliated with this one too?

Detective Hunter turned to Bancroft with drudgery eyes.

"He's coming for more!"

CHAPTER SIX

WHEN SERIAL ATTACKS GROW into serial murders, the investigation is expected to take a different turn. More hands are gathered and more guts are deployed. The attacker raised the bar for Detective Hunter and Bancroft with an egregious murder on a Friday morning.

Bancroft stood at the apartment entrance, his heart pounding in his chest. The air was thick with an eerie silence, broken only by the distant sound of sirens echoing through the streets of Capeton. He took a deep breath and stepped inside, prepared to face the grim reality that awaited him.

Are there many more to come?

The apartment was fully lit and the curtains were drawn entirely. The atmosphere was heavy with the scent of fear and the lingering stench of violence. Bancroft cautiously moved through the space, his eyes scanning every corner for clues. He couldn't afford to miss a single detail.

The living room was awful. Both nights the attacker visited him, it flushed Bancroft's head with his room images. Furniture lay overturned, glass shards scattered across the floor like shattered dreams. The walls were marred with blood splatters, painting a macabre portrait of the brutality that had unfolded within these walls. Bancroft approached the bloodstains, his gloved hand reaching out to touch the sticky crimson residue.

He couldn't get himself to touch it. Every single investigator is cautious about crime scene contamination. Besides, he saw clearly that the forensics team was still in action. But at least studying it keenly won't temper with it.

Examining the patterns, Bancroft noted the trajectory of the blood spatter. It was evident that the victim had been attacked with great force. Laying side by side the visual image of how fierce his two-time attack was, he suggested that the attacker must have unleashed a savage frenzy of blows. The violence must have been unforgiving. It was a stark reminder that the attacker has always been intentional about his strikes.

As Bancroft moved further into the apartment, he entered the kitchen. The scene here was no less gruesome. The tiled floor was slick with blood, footprints leaving a trail of crimson evidence. He followed the tracks, his eyes narrowing as he discovered a discarded knife hidden among the scattered utensils.

The murder weapon told its own story. The serrated blade was stained with blood, its edges dulled by the forceful impact. Bancroft drew the attention of the nearby forensic team member who bagged the knife, preserving it as evidence and for further testing.

Leaving the kitchen, Bancroft ascended the stairs, the weight of the investigation heavy on his shoulders. It was slowly becoming a downward spiral. The upstairs hallway was fairly lit, the creaking floorboards whispering secrets of the past. He approached the bedroom door, his hand trembling slightly as he turned the knob.

Inside the bedroom, the air hung heavy with a suffocating dread. The room was in disarray, the mattress overturned and sheets twisted in a struggle for survival. According to Mrs Palmer, that was where it all began. Bancroft noticed signs of a desperate struggle, and furniture shifted to fend off the attacker.

The son of a bitch uses one exact pattern. He thought. He saw that the attacker used his physical power to sap the life out of unlucky victims who couldn't stage a matching resistance to his strength.

In the corner of the room, Bancroft spotted a shattered mirror. He carefully examined the broken fragments, his eyes catching a reflection—a glimpse of the terror that had consumed Mr Palmer in his final moments. Each shard held a distorted image of the truth, a fragmented puzzle waiting to be pieced together.

Outside the apartment, on a trolley, lay the remains of Mr Palmer, wrapped in a nylon body bag. Bancroft once glanced at it before sludging into the apartment. This time, he needed to take a closer look. A member of the medic team zipped it open at the expense of a nod from Bancroft.

His face contorted in a frown. Bancroft studied the still body, the sight sending a shiver to the edge of his spine. Mr. Palmer's potbelly had watered down and his topaz skin grew pale and frigid. His chubby face had long begun to wriggle—it became a mask of terror, frozen right from the final moments of his existence. To Bancroft', the scene was in some way, a haunting reminder of the fragility of life and the suddenness with which it could be snuffed out at the flick of a finger.

As Bancroft caught a glimpse of Mrs Palmer from a distance, his grief shot up. The deceased, Mr Palmer, was a court clerk in the famous Cedar Magistrate Court at Route 47. She taught in an elementary school up the hills of Vermouth Lane. The two married for seventeen years before the attacker took Mr Palmer's life away.

Bancroft recollected how sorrow and pain found permanent succour in her eyes. They weren't not reddened but held crumbs of pain and agony. He had spoken with her earlier and he waltzed closer to the apartment entrance where she stood with who could be some sympathizer. Their conversation came alive in his head.

He had approached her gently, and his voice filled with empathy. "Mrs Palmer, I understand this is a challenging time for you, but I need you to be strong as we try to get to the root of this. We need your strength to go further; you must tell us what you know when we need you."

He'd also recall when he asked her what she saw. "Can you tell me what you saw during the attack?"

Tears welled up in her eyes as she recalled the horrifying events. "I-Uhm," she sobbed, wiping her face with her palms. "I heard a commotion downstairs," she began, her voice trembling amid the low sob. "I rushed down to see what was happening, and that's when I saw a masked man attacking my husband."

"Did you get any closer?" Bancroft had asked.

"I-I-I tried to intervene, but he struck me, injuring my arm," he lifted her blood-stained bandaged arm for Bancroft to see.

"Did you see this figure, Mrs Palmer?"
She nodded in the negative. "I barely saw his face through the darkness, but he was tall and wore dark clothing."

Bancroft had nodded, jotting down notes as Mrs Palmer spoke. "Thank you, Mrs. Palmer. We'll do everything we can to find the person responsible for this. Please take care of yourself and rest assured that we're working tirelessly to bring justice to your husband."

Mrs Palmer nodded, her eyes filled with gratitude and sorrow. "Thank you, Detective Bancroft. Please find the monster who did this. Scott didn't deserve to die like this."

Bancroft nodded in response. Despite the chaos, he wondered how a detective got into his title. Well, he couldn't be so blown away. He was doing only what detectives do. He was ready to back out. Not when Capeton PD has no problem with his involvement in the investigation.

Bancroft is no forensic expert, but he saw a daunting need to examine the body without touching or documenting anything. That job was out of his league. He noticed the wounds. They were profound and severe, evidence of a frenzied attack. One of the wounds sat on Mr Palmer's chest, stretching as far as his upper left ribs. The extreme tear and drag made it evident that Mr Palmer wasn't a walk-over—he perhaps gave the attacker some tough time. Yet, the gutful murderer showed the court clerk no mercy, leaving behind a brutal display of power and malice.

The murder scene painted a gruesome picture close to what Bancroft had seen. It could be at the battle in Havana or somewhere within the service in the Navy. He pocketed the thought and wambled away out of the building.

He can't get away with this!

When he spotted someone from a distance, Bancroft was engulfed in a conversation with Detective Hunter, who took the time to examine the building equally. He saw the figure by the side but remained confident that it was who he thought it was. Under no circumstances did he feel he could mistake that familiar posture for somebody else's.

Detective Elaine Murphy.
"A hungry hawk following another smoke, I guess," Bancroft grumbled as he shuffled closer to her. Detective Elaine shooed off the medic man she was talking to and dipped her hands into the pockets of her black leather jacket, and her lips curved in a sly smile as she stroked her jet-black to the back.

"You're right, Bancroft. We all are chasing the same smoke maker. I'm just a new hawk in a new territory. Does that make us any different?" Elaine said under her breath, looking over her shoulder.

"We've never been on the same train, Elaine. I don't chase rainbows!" Bancroft shrieked.

"At least we both are chasing this smoke," she said carelessly, her eyes shot ahead, right in the direction of the steaming ambulance.

"Don't make me think this is another of your pranks, Elaine," Bancroft accused, gawking at her diamond-shaped face.

"You've got the first murder of many more to come in your territory and you call that a prank?"

"What do you mean the murder of many more?"

"Serial murder attempts rarely end in a lone murder. It's a serial perhaps, and he'd come back for me?"

"Enough of your mind games. What are you talking about? Many more to come? What makes you think I am not tempted to see your hands in all these?"

Detective Elaine lurched her head backwards and smiled again. "You barely know me, Bancroft."

"But I know you know so much you're not supposed to…"

"Then…"

"Prove how you got your hands on this intelligence Bancroft barked.

Elaine adjusted her posture, buried her face in her arms and paced back and forth, stealing glances in Detective Hunter's direction. She grabbed a pack of cigarettes from her pocket and lit a stick. Bancroft didn't see that coming. He drifted a bit away when the scent from Detective Elaine's first puff poisoned the air.

"You can't come around here, show up at my crime scenes, interrogate my witnesses and think I'm gonna let that slide…"

"I'm only trying to help, Bancroft. I-I have no idea why that's some big deal…"

"It is a big deal, and you clout chaser," a third voice behind Bancroft echoed, startling them.

Detective Elaine trashed the stick of cigarettes and stepped on it. Her hand stretched forward, "Detective Elaine Murphy. Montebello PD," she said.

"Spare me the pleasantries. I know who you are," Detective Hunter announced, standing akimbo as her hand hung in the air. "And I know that you have no place in Capeton! What are you doing here?"

Detective Elaine furrowed her brows as she retrieved her hand in disappointment. "I'm only here to help, Detective!"

"Because we are incompetent, I guess."

"We both know that's what I mean. Come on…I…"

"Don't you think you should speak for yourself? I know not what you know and whatever it is you know, take them back to your PD. They need it more than we do!" Detective Hunter aired, his face contorted into a hard.

Detective Elaine rolled her eyes, wondering what he thought she knew. Perhaps, she felt Bancroft must have told him all she shared with him at the club.

"This is…"

"Good cops don't beg for cases, Elaine," he cut her in. "They earn it!"

Detective Hunter waited for the words you sink in before he added his last statement. "We don't need you in Capeton, Elaine."

As soon as Detective Hunter bashed out of them, knocking Elaine's shoulder as he walked past her, Bancroft adjusted his shirt and inched closer to Elaine who stood still and unbothered. "If you think I'm gonna buy all the cheap shit you said back at the club, you're some big joke. You're interfering in a full-blown criminal investigation and might bite more than you can chew…"

"I'm a cop, Bancroft…"

"In your damn town. Not here. You have no place here, Elaine," Detective Hunter hollered, surprised at how loud his voice rose. He had stopped, listened to what Bancroft said and as his voice droned the air, he spun around to be sure no one noticed their fight.
He shuffled towards them and glanced right into Elaine's contorted face. "Stay out of this or I'll write to your PD," he threatened.

"We can always find better ways to do this, Hunter…"

"There's no room for negotiation. If you're a cop as you claim, you should know that crisscrossing jurisdiction is nothing to condone…"

"But…"

"Get out of my town," Detective Hunter yelled, his voice filled with venom.

Detective Elaine Murphy's face remained calm, a smile playing at the corners of her lips. "Every dog has its day," she retorted, leaving the scene with an air of defiance.

Bancroft watched her departure, and his mind clouded with suspicion. He couldn't shake the feeling that there was more to this case than met the eye, that secrets were hidden within the shadows of Capeton. He felt Detective Elaine hold a flicker of them too.

Who is next?

What does he want?

These questions echoed in his mind, fueling his determination to uncover the truth and end the reign of terror as he watched Detective Elaine sashay out of sight with her sleek shape.

As Bancroft stood alone in the murder scene, surrounded by the remnants of violence, he knew the answers lay buried within the darkness. Capeton was a city on the edge, and he would be its shield against the encroaching storm of evil.

But.

Who's next?

CHAPTER SEVEN

BANCROFT STOOD IN THE LIVING ROOM, his body tense with anticipation. The room felt suffocating, the air heavy with their escalating disagreement. Rachel's eyes bore into his, and her voice laced with fear and frustration.

He was losing it.

She was losing.

The room was flaming up.

"Bancroft, I can't just stand by and watch you throw yourself into danger," Rachel pleaded, her voice quivering with emotion.

"What danger are you talking about?" Bancroft chimed in, taming his tone as much as he could.

"This investigation is getting out of control. I can't afford to see you get stuck right at the centre of the crossfire. I don't want to lose you, Bancroft. Can't you see that?"

Bancroft clenched his fists, and his voice laced with determination. He paced back and forth, stealing a steady glance at Rachel. "Listen to me. I understand your concern...I mean, I-I get that you have my best interest at heart but can't you see it? It's too late to say no!"

"You're not a fucking cop, Bancroft. The attacker can be found and convicted with just a little of your help and not you right at the helm of affairs."

"I'm not at the helm of affairs, Rachel. Detective Hunter is..."

"Well, that's not what it seems! You always show up, contacting these victims in real-time even more than some cops do...I mean, acting like nothing else matters to you!"

Bancroft lurched closer, trying to close the distance between him and the agitated Rachel, but she was too pissed to let him get close enough. "This might be too hard, but I can't back down now. We can't let fear dictate our actions. I have to protect the innocent and fight for justice. I won't walk away from that responsibility."

Rachel's eyes welled up with tears as she stepped closer, desperation etched across her face. She was the one now initiating the body contact. "But Bancroft, you're not trained for this."

"I'm a former Navy SEAL for crying out loud. What other training do I need to go after injustice with all I've got within me?"

"Even when it means risking your life? For a cause that's not even yours? The Capeton PD can handle it. They're equipped for this. You're just putting yourself, putting me, in the line of fire."

Bancroft shook his head, his voice firm. "This is personal now, Rachel. The attacks started with me. I can't ignore that. I won't stand by while innocent lives are at stake. I refuse to be a bystander when I have the power to make a difference."

Rachel's voice cracked as she reached out, her hand trembling. "I can't lose you, Bancroft. I love you and can't bear the thought of something happening to you. There's more to life than this relentless pursuit of justice. We have each other, and that should be enough."

Can just me and she be enough for me? Bancroft thought, flickering his brows. His eyes softened as he reached out to cup Rachel's face, his voice filled with tenderness and conviction.

"Rachel, I love you too but can't turn my back on what's right. We can't let fear control us. We have to face evil head-on, no matter the risks. I'm willing to fight for what I believe in, even if it means walking through fire."

The room grew silent, the tension thick in the air. Rachel's tears flowed freely now. Her voice choked with anger and desperation. She drifted backwards and stood akimbo, her face squeezing into a grotesque grimace. "You're so stubborn, Bancroft. It's like you're slowly walking yourself to hell. Can't you see that?"

Bancroft felt a pang of hurt pierce his heart as he recoiled from her words. He stepped back, his eyes searching Rachel's face for any signs of remorse or understanding.

"I might not be a homicide detective like Detective Hunter, but I know that fighting crimes do not give the leeway for carelessness. We tread cautiously and act in line with the provisions of the Police laws that predict what we do. This is a normal procedure."

"These things are rarely what they seem like," Rachel added.

"Most things disguise but you'll never know until you try."

"I bet this doesn't make sense in crime-fighting. It has always been a chase of you guys biting off more than you can chew."

Bancroft seemed moved by her frequent emphasis on the complexity of the case. She was concerned that he felt the itch to reconsider the suspicions he had always been pocketing.

"Rachel, you sound like you know more than we do. Is there something you're not telling me?"

Rachel's expression shifted from anger to fear, her eyes darting around the room as if searching for an escape. Her voice stammered, her words barely audible. "I...I can't...I can't do this right now." With that, she turned on her heel and rushed out of the apartment, leaving Bancroft stunned, confused, and apprehensive.

Bancroft's mind raced as the door slammed shut, trying to understand what had happened. There was an undeniable sense that Rachel knew more than she was letting on, that secrets were hidden beneath her evasive words and actions. His instincts told him there was a connection, that the attacks were not random but somehow tied to their lives.

Taking a deep breath, Bancroft pushed aside the emotional turmoil and refocused on the task. Capeton was a city on the brink, and he had a duty to protect its inhabitants. His chosen path was treacherous, but he would walk it with unwavering resolve, even if it meant facing the darkness alone.

If only the enemy eventually gets generous enough to leave tracks behind.

But what if he lives with the enemy?

Days turned into weeks as Bancroft tried to reach Rachel, but she remained distant, avoiding his calls and messages. The rift between them grew wider, fuelled by the unspoken tension and unanswered questions. He found himself questioning their relationship, the foundation on which it was built, and the uncertainties that had come to the surface.

He had always left questions on the table. But this time, they had doubled and grown more convincing by the day. Their love wasn't just getting sore and on the verge of rotting.

Bancroft spent countless hours poring over what he felt was evidence connecting the dots and analysing the patterns. Right from his days as a Navy SEAL, he's banked on his instincts on my hormone-influenced actions and now, it was getting more useful than ever. His mind became consumed with the investigation, his obsession driving him to push forward despite mounting obstacles. He couldn't shake the feeling that there was more at play, that the truth was lurking beneath the surface.

Not too far anymore. He couldn't tell where and how he'd get his hand around it but could feel it.

All he wished was to keep pushing and then sit back and see how things peter out.

In the depths of the night, as he studied the case files littered on his worktable, the memories of their argument played an endless loop in his mind. It is like one of his favourite country tracks booming from his huge tweeters on repeat. The pain of Rachel's words lingered. As Rachel claimed, it didn't smear his heart with thoughts of backing out and letting the right people do their jobs. Rather, the echoes of her nags fueled his flair to uncover the secrets she held.

After the fight, she dashed into the night's heat and never returned. Four nights came and gone but she still didn't seem okay to take his calls or reply to his texts. Perhaps, her irritation had hit the roof. Possibly, she now hated him more than a psycho in a psychic home who does hate a psychiatrist priest who's always with the syringe containing the sleeping substance. Bancroft knew he had to find and confront her once and for all.

Find her. I must find her!

One evening, unable to bear the weight of the dreadful uncertainty any longer, Bancroft drove to Rachel's apartment. After stalking her at the club for days without any hope of ever getting to see her, a colleague tipped him off to her whereabouts. Squeezing a ruffled bill into the informant's hand was all he needed to get all the details. He knew where Rachel lived. He had been there a couple of times. He only needed to be told exactly when she'd pull her rickety Sedan into the tiny garage of the building.

His heart raced as he approached the door, anticipation and anxiety warring. Deep within him was a sturdy gamble — a bamboozle within the core of his being, fighting to decide if he was to go in for peace or take things hard on her. Perhaps, the harder he'd get, the easier she might say something. He settled for none. He dreaded staying on the fence but it was the best thing for him to do then. He left whatever that'd come in to be determined by Racheal's reaction to his illegal visit.

With a trembling hand, he knocked, the sound echoing through the empty hallway. Room 302. He knew he was at the right place. He couldn't miss it for anything under the sun.

The door creaked open, revealing Rachel standing there, her eyes red and puffy, her face pale and gaunt. She looked at Bancroft, her voice barely above a whisper. "What do you want, Bancroft?"

He blinked and heaved a silent sight as his voice faltered momentarily, his emotions bubbling to the surface. "Rachel, we need to talk."

She stepped into the hallway, scanning it with a fine-tooth comb in both directions. Perhaps, he felt Bancroft had grown so obsessed with working with the law enforcement agencies that he could pull over at her door in the company of some annoying black or sunburnt cop on mufti.

She gawked at his tired frame and slammed him with the statement he had long expected to hear. "We have nothing to talk about, Bancroft."

"Come on," Bancroft stepped further, his legs a few inches into the room. "We can't let this come between us. I need to know the truth. I need to understand what's happening."

Rachel's eyes flickered with a mix of pain and regret. "What truth?"

"Can I at least come in?" Bancroft asked, completely ignoring her question.

She let him in. He made it to the couch and slumped into it. He could feel extreme dryness on the walls of his throat but kept putting. He knew Rachel was too mad to offer him at least a glass of water. And he wasn't ready to ask for one either.

She sat opposite him, her legs crossed and her eyes resting on Bancroft'. "What brought you to my place without prior notice!"

"We both know you've been avoiding me like a plague…"

"Oh. A plague? And what makes you think you are not?"

Bancroft didn't answer that question. Not like he never wanted but he had no reasonable response. At least one that won't negatively offset the tempo between them. He craved absolute ease between. That's the only way he'd get Rachel to talk.

"Tell me what you know, Rachel."

"What makes you think I know something?"

He flung his hands into the air. "You're too smart not to."

Rachel chuckled. "Your investigative pickup lines could work magic when used on actual witnesses. Not me. Why do I feel like you're interrogating me?"

Bancroft drifted to the edge of the couch, his tone shooting up a bit. "I'm not interrogating you, Rachel...I've got nothing on me. No recorder. No notepad. Nothing."

Rachel smiled. "As if you'd let me know if you have a diminutive recording device implanted into your cloth."

Silence hovered over them briefly before Bancroft pleaded for answers again.

"Bancroft, I... I can't. It's too dangerous. I can't put you at risk. You need to let this go."

Progress! Bancroft saw progress!

He shook his head, and determination etched into every line of his face. "I can't let it go, Rachel. This is tearing us apart. I need to know what you're hiding. We're in this together, remember? I won't walk away until I have the answers we deserve."

Once again, silence hung in the air, heavy with unspoken truths. Rachel's eyes darted away, her voice trembling. "There are things you don't understand, Bancroft. Things I can't explain right now. But you have to trust me. Trust that I'm doing what's best for us."

Bancroft's frustration boiled over, his voice rising with anger and desperation. "Trust? How can I trust you when you won't tell me the truth? I've seen the signs, Rachel. I know there's more to this than meets the eye. If you don't tell me, I'll find the answers myself."

Rachel's eyes widened, fear flashing across her face. "No, Bancroft! You don't understand. You're walking into something far more dangerous than you can imagine. I'm trying to protect you, to keep you safe."

"Did you say you want to protect me?" Bancroft queried, substituting his low tone for something slightly higher.

The room fell into an uneasy silence as the weight of their words hung heavy in the air. Bancroft's mind raced between his love for Rachel and his unrelenting pursuit of the truth. The darkness outside mirrored his turmoil; he knew he had reached a critical crossroads.

"Keeping the truth from you is the only way I can protect you, Bancroft!" Rachel stressed. She was off the couch and making back-and-forth movements around the couch.

"What is it, you know, Rachel?" Bancroft asked again. The ease on his face was long gone. Perhaps, he lost his patience and his tolerance was drastically running dry.

She mopped her face with her palms. "I can't say!"

Bancroft pulled a fake chuckle. "Listen, Rachel. I do not work for Capeton PD but I have a voice there. I can subpoena you and you end up saying all you know before many more eyes…more cops, journalists, newsmen and a jury who won't let you breathe until you spit every word you know!"

Rachel chuckled. "Whatever way you find pleasing. Go ahead. I ain't falling for that cheap threat!"

"I'm not threatening you. I'm only telling what the cops might be forced to do if they find out you know something but won't say it!"

"And how will they know that I do know something? If this conversation isn't recorded and listened to by your godforsaken partner in some backdoor out there, no one's gonna come for me!"

"You think I won't?"

"You lack the balls, Bancroft."

With a heavy heart, Bancroft turned and walked away, the sound of Rachel's voice fading into the night. He couldn't shake the feeling that he was losing her, that their once-unbreakable bond was shattering before his eyes. At the same time, he didn't only wonder what she was hiding and how valuable it could be to the investigation. He equally wondered how weak she thought he was. How soft she had been taking him for. He felt sad that she didn't know the ways of a man trained to kill, maim and destroy whatever looked evil and could harm innocent people.

He had every reason to go hard on Bancroft. To deploy a means you have her talk to him before he gets Capeton PD involved. He wanted to weigh what she knew and perhaps, find a better way to keep her off the radar if things go south. He had no reason to do that. But he knew he still loved her. That was the reason behind his leniency towards her.

He couldn't abandon his principles, his unwavering commitment to justice or punch love in the face. Yet, the raw desire to know the truth beckoned him, pulling him deeper into the heart of uneasiness and confusion.

A few more hours after returning from Rachel's place, Bancroft was trapped on the leather-quilted armchair on his workstation, sifting through case files in his cluttered office when a knock on the door reeled his attention. He looked up, his eyes meeting the gaze of Detective Elaine Murphy, a sense of tension radiating from her. Bancroft rose from his chair, wary yet curious.

How did she find my apartment?

"What are you doing in my apartment?" Bancroft asked, his voice tinged with caution.

Detective Murphy stepped further into the room, her eyes scanning the disarrayed workspace. "Bancroft, we need to talk. I've been following the recent developments in the case, and I think it's time we set aside our differences and work together."

"That hasn't answered my question?" Bancroft thundered again.

"What are you talking about?" Detective Elaine stressed.

"How did you find me?"

Detective Elaine chuckled. "I'm a fucking cop, Bancroft. I mean, we have our ways around these things. Besides, why sound so surprised when you live in an enlisted apartment in Capeton? Anyone out there can locate you at the expense of a Google search."

Bancroft raised an eyebrow, scepticism and intrigue flickering across his face. He agreed with her. He wasn't too hard to find. Not like he even felt it was necessary to want some sort of privacy, like unlisted phone lines and an apartment off the housing registry.

"What do you want to talk about?" Bancroft asked.

"Don't you think a glass of Vodka would be a good way to set the atmosphere for this talk?" Detective Elaine asked, putting his absolute refusal to give her a good guest treatment before him.

"I do not offer drinks to guests. Not a type like you!" he growled.

Gawking at the wine pantry opposite her, Detective Elaine hoisted, framed, and made forward. "Sometimes, we must get what we want all by ourselves."

Bancroft slumped to the couch as clanks of glasses droned through the sitting room. Detective Elaine reshuffled towards the centre table with two whiskey-filled margarita glasses. She wanted Vodka. Perhaps, she settled for Whiskey after she couldn't Vodka. Bancroft wished she knew that he dreaded Russian gins.

"I got you a glass," she said, dropping the glass before him. She plonked her frame back into the couch and took a long sip of her glass.

"I'm sure you didn't cover four miles to come and serve yourself a glass of Whiskey in my house. What's this show all about, Elaine?"

"When I got into the Police Academy. I had a drill master known for one weird statement," Detective Elaine began. Bancroft knew he wasn't ready for some cock and bull story but he had to let her land. At least to make her feel comfortable. "I never saw sense in it until I switched to the homicide unit four years ago. The enemy gets more appetite when there's an evil among the same people chasing him for his evil."

Bancroft kept mute, intentionally refusing to make meaning from what she had just said. Even if he did, it was stuck in his head.

"Do you know what that means?" she asked, sipping from her glass again.

"Not like it matters to me. But, you can come out plain if you want to," Bancroft gruffed.

"We can't get to these people if we play cat and dog. That's the evil in us. It spurs the guts of the people we're supposed to bring to a book. It only makes them get stronger."

"There's nothing wrong with joining forces to take out a threat but there's always a procedure to follow… ethics binds us…all designed to protect us."

"No matter the urgency of the situation?"

"What are you insinuating, Elaine?"

"Something very simple. To hell with ethics and save a life. That's what cops are supposed to do!"

"Why the sudden change of heart, Detective?" Bancroft cut in, completely digressing from their conversation.

"What do you mean by that?" she queried.

"Last time we crossed paths, you couldn't wait to see my back!"

Detective Elaine's gaze hardened, her voice taking on a steely edge. "I may not agree with your methods, Bancroft, but I can't deny that you have an uncanny knack for uncovering the truth. We need all the help we can get. This case is far bigger than any of us could imagine."

Bancroft nodded. The tension in the room was palpable. "I've been digging deep, Detective. Some secrets and connections go beyond what we've uncovered. The closer I get to the truth, the more dangerous it becomes. I won't back down."

Detective Murphy's eyes met Bancroft's with determination and caution. "Bancroft, there are forces at play here that you can't begin to comprehend. This goes deeper than any of us can fathom. Be careful who you trust, and watch your back."

Bancroft's jaw tightened, his resolve hardening. "I appreciate the warning, Detective. But where's all these leading to? What do you want from me? Or is it the PD you want?"

Detective Elaine pulled a smile. Even the furniture could tell that it was fake. "I want nobody. Not you. Not the PD. I just want to help. That's all!"

Bancroft's expression softened slightly, a hint of understanding in his eyes. "I can see the fire burning within you. I can see that you wanna help but not me nor the PD would take in any crap you claim you know! Damn, the Jennifer Alvarez shit. That's what Hunter needs. That's what I need. That's what the Chief himself might need!"

Without a word, Detective Elaine emptied her glass. Stationed before the door, her hands a few inches away from the doorknob, she swung in Bancroft's direction.

"No one ever got lucky to find proof of my claims because no one ever asked. Not you. Not the PD. Not even the fat-ass Hunter who can barely hunt down a deer, let alone a specialist assailant. I wonder how he got that name."

Bancroft shuffled ahead, his hands buried in the pockets of his pants. "A jury's verdict is preceded by the amount of proof of crime the execution counsel can place before the court. That's the means to an end," he paused and then grabbed a hat off his coat rack. "Show us proof of how you got what you claim you know. Name names, places, things, then no one's gonna walk you out of our strategy room. Even if everybody does, I won't!"

"That's what you think my passcode is?" she asked him in an extremely low tone...something close to a whisper.

"I can be an overthinker. But that's not a thought. It's a fact!"
Detective Elaine grabbed the doorknob harder. But, this time, he slammed the door shut. Her eyes flickered as she waltzed towards Bancroft who towered a few meters away.

"Is it also a fact that you might want more than facts and proof from me? Is it?"

Bancroft kept mute and remained still. Detective Elaine was closer now. More than he thought was necessary. He could feel her Whiskey-riven breath as she sniffed him from his chest upward.

"I can do more than you'll ever think I can to prove that divided, our target gets stronger but together, his guts will fade away like a dark cloud being dismantled by the harsh rays of the afternoon sun."

When her hands stretched beyond its jurisdiction, Bancroft grabbed it firmly. His teeth clenched and his other hand bared.

"Up for negotiations, Elaine. But not this! Step away from me," Bancroft bulged.

She smiled devilishly. The smile had this way of reminding Bancroft of Rachel. As a stripper, she knew exactly how she could get to the weakest point of a man and beg him to get down on her just by body movement, gestures and tongue-wagging. He couldn't afford to watch Detective Elaine deploy the same trick on him.

Bancroft shoved her aside as her hands went down further in a powerful yank that got her hankering for balance. "Leave now!" Bancroft hollered.

Still smiling, she walked towards the door. Bancroft was up to watch her moving until she was completely out of sight. But then, the bell went. It wasn't the bell on his bedside table. It was the doorbell.

He visited no Rachel. No Detective Elaine visited him. The pain in his head was enough to tell him everything.

Did I just dream again?

CHAPTER EIGHT

THE WALLS OF THE INTERROGATION ROOM seemed to close in as Detective Hunter took the lead in questioning Otis Crane.

The sober Otis Crane sat across the table, his reddened eyes buried deep within their sockets as he kept still, waiting for the next line of questions from Detective Hunter who was whispering to a third voice outside the interrogation room.

Bancroft's thoughts when he first saw Otis and pondered over his involvement in the case didn't change. Stealing another stripping look at the fifty-four-year-old man, more thoughts flashed through his head.

To Bancroft, Otis didn't seem like it. Not one bit. His once robust frame was now reduced to a weak and feeble figure. His greying hair was dishevelled, and deep lines etched his weathered face, telling tales of a life marked by hardships and sorrow. His frail shoulders hunched forward as if bearing the world's weight while his trembling hands nervously fidgeted with a worn-out handkerchief. He exuded an air of vulnerability, a man who had seen better days and was caught in a merciless investigation.

His eyes, perhaps, once full of vitality, now held a glimmer of fear and weariness. They darted anxiously around the room, avoiding direct contact with Bancroft's penetrating gaze. When he first spoke before Detective Hunter got interrupted by the voice at the door, his voice was soft and quivered with each word, reflecting his frailty. Every sentence seemed to be accompanied by a hesitant pause as if he were carefully considering his response or struggling to recall the events under scrutiny.

The lines on his forehead deepened as the weight of his guilt or innocence pressed upon him, making him feel smaller and more vulnerable in the face of the detective's relentless questioning.

At the same time, Bancroft couldn't help but bring to the foreground that the same Otis Crane does work his ass out in the wood farm, lifting nine-kilogram professional-grade chainsaws for hours without winding out in exhaustion. *Or does he?*

After his DNA was rediscovered at the murder scene of the boy at the train station, he became a major suspect whose arrest needed no warrant. He was napped in the middle of the tree farm by 4 pm and transferred to Capeton PD for questioning.

As Detective Hunter finished with the man at the door, the air grew thick with tension as he sat across Otis again, his intimidating face staring through the man's tired eyes.

His coarse baritone came alive, sharp, and unwavering. "Otis Crane. First, we had substantial evidence linking you to three serial attacks within Capeton," Detective Hunter broke the silence.

"My son told me about your visit, and I phoned to clarify. I know nothing about these attacks!" Otis defended, his voice coming up every time he tried speaking. He was recovering.

"And that isn't all, Mr Crane! You saw it on the news, I guess. But, I'm gonna do you the honour of familiarising you with the case."

"That's not necessary," Otis bloated, turning to Bancroft.

Bancroft and Detective Hunter traded blank glances.

"Why?" Detective Hunter asked.

"I saw the news! I've never missed a day."

"And you've grasped every detail about them. Right?"

Otis hissed. "Not like a newscaster who wants to talk about it on TV would. But yes!"

Detective Hunter clapped and then rifled files onto the table. Some were placed in flat files while others were in big brown envelopes. "Well then. That'd save us more time!"

"I didn't do any of these. Just let me go back to my family."

Detective Hunter ignored him. Bancroft wasn't too surprised but at least he was beginning to see signs that Otis's energy didn't match his appearance. He looked weak but sounded strong. Bancroft just watched with his arms folded. He didn't want to make assumptions. Not just yet.

Detective Hunter handed Crane the first big brown envelope. He nodded approval for him to open it and then waited till he began rifling pictures of it one after the other.

"On July 5th at exactly 10:43 pm, a masked man attacked," Detective Hunter turned to Bancroft "Bancroft Logan in his apartment at Maryland Avenue.

Of course, you can see the ruins in the picture beyond what the censored media will ever tell you."

There was silence as Crane pored over the pictures. Detective Hunter continued, liking the silence. "Two days later, Bancroft got attacked again. It's 11:05 pm, fifteen minutes later than the previous attack. More damage was done."

Detective Hunter briefly dropped another document on the table. This time, it's not an envelope. It's a flat file. He flunked it open and ditched it towards Crane.

"His name is Scot Palmer. A court clerk at the Magistrate Court at route 47. He was murdered on a Friday morning. Battered. Bloodied. Left to bleed from the brain."

"How then does all these point to me?" Crane asked, his face contorted in a frown.

"This," Detective Hunter answered, placing another photo on the table. Beside it are two other papers. One looks like an x-ray film and the other is like some test result. "DNA match results. Your DNA was found at these three crime scenes."

"And..."

"That could only mean one thing, Mr Crane!"

"I murdered them?"

"Murdered once and attacked twice if that's what you mean. But that was never how I'd have put it if you had let me land!"

"Then land!"

"You've helped me do that already. You mentioned murdering them and you just go ahead and tell me if it's true!"

Furious. "You cops must be insane!" he growled, his countenance swinging into something Hunter and Bancroft never saw coming.

Watching all the drama unfold, Bancroft was sure they didn't need a psychiatrist to ascertain that Crane must be a living alibi. He looked like a pauper but had the energy of a berserker. Bancroft wondered what it'd feel like to get in a fight with him.

"There's no need to pick a fight, Mr Crane," Detective Hunter tried taming the situation. "There's always a way out of every mess. Either you agree that you attacked Bancroft twice and murdered Mr Scot Palmer if you did it. But, if you didn't, tell me you didn't!"

"What would I want to murder someone? What am I supposed to gain from that?"

Detective Hunter shrugged, unsure of how to respond.

"So, you didn't attack Bancroft Logan on July 5th at about 10: 47 pm?" Detective Hunter asked.

"I did not!"

"How about the next attack...three days after the first?"

"I know nothing about that! Nothing will prompt me to harm Bancroft!"

"How about Mr Palmer's murder?"

Crane nodded his head. "I have no idea where he lives nor what he looked like before seeing the photos you gave me."

"Why do we find your DNA in these crime scenes, Mr Crane?"
"I can't say. Are you sure this test result is real?"

Detective Hunter chuckled. "DNA test doesn't lie. Our intricate team of technicians runs repeated tests on these samples. The results never get any different. It's you and always you!"

"So, my DNA being seen around there means I was the murderer?"

"Listen, Mr. Crane. Forensic science has developed over the centuries. Except we don't get our hands on these specimens, our results don't mislead or lie. Finding your DNA on a crime scene through your fingerprints and footprint could mean two things; You committed the crime. You were an accomplice or at the crime and can say who committed it!"

"But none of these align with. Before the crime, I had to idea where these people lived. I did know they existed. How can I possibly be at these crime scenes."

"Then, there's something you're not willing to share!"
Otis' eyes widened with shock and disbelief as the reality of his situation sunk in. He felt his heart race, his palms growing clammy as he struggled to find words to defend himself. "Detective, you have to believe me. I had nothing to do with those murders. I swear, I was at work in Dream Farms wood farm during the hours of those heinous acts."

"Well. Perfect alibi. Your neighbours witnessed you either at home or out with your family within the time frame of these murders. But are good murderers not perfect pretenders?"

"I have no pretence. You've asked my kids. My wife. My neighbours. Who else are you supposed to confirm my whereabouts on the nights of these acts?"

Detective Hunter's face remained stern, his voice filled with determination and scepticism. "Your alibi may hold up, but the physical evidence doesn't lie, Mr. Crane. We found your DNA multiple times at the crime scenes. How do you explain that?"

Crane shifted uncomfortably in his seat, racing to find a plausible explanation. "I... I don't know, Detective. I can't explain how my DNA ended up there."

A noise was heard at the door. It was for Detective Hunter. He retrieved the cups of steaming coffee and made them for the table. One for him and the other for Bancroft. He turned to the frustrated Crane.

"Even in the least competent court, you can't get away with this sweeping evidence against you. How do you think your attorney can manoeuvre you out of it?"

"Someone must have planted them," Crane said sharply.

Bancroft stole a glance at Hunter and they both kept put.

"You think someone framed me for these murders," Detective Hunter asked emphatically.

"That's the only reasonable explanation to how my DNA can be found on crime scenes I've never been to?"
Detective Hunter's gaze hardened, suspicion seeping into his voice. He paused for a few seconds after sipping from his cup of coffee.

"So, you can't think of anything else? As you got there but didn't commit the crime or you might know someone who did?"

"All of those don't fall in. I never went to those places nor saw any of these victims except on TV!"

"You saw some of them on TV?"

Crane nodded a yes. His mouth shut tight.

"Like which of them?"

Crane turned to Bancroft. "Bancroft Logan."

Bancroft lowered his head, walking towards the mahogany cupboard behind them.

"Back to your suggestion earlier. Do you have any enemies, anyone with a motive to ruin your life?"

Crane stammered, his voice tinged with fear and frustration. "There's this man, Victor Thompson. We used to work together at the lumber yard. We had a fallout a while ago, and things have never been the same since. He always resented me and blamed me for his failures. I think he'd have been out to get me, to destroy my life but…"

"But what?"

"He died a year ago!"

Detective Hunter exchanged a glance with Bancroft, a flicker of recognition passing between them. Victor Thompson's name had come up in Detective Hunter's previous investigations. It was an incident that later did seem like a crime at all. All leads were dead-ends. He told Bancroft about it in detail.

The case was an accident dismissed as irrelevant but with the disguise of *natural death; drunk driving.* Victor Thompson was drunk. Heavy alcohol was detected in his tracts in an autopsy a few minutes after he crashed into the electric pole. But Detective Hunter had to try his luck. He turned to Bancroft who must have been itching to talk and nodded towards the staring Crane.

The two have worked together enough for Bancroft to understand what that meant. He nodded back and took the first sip off his coffee mug.

Bancroft leaned closer to Crane, his voice filled with urgency and curiosity. "What do you know about Thompson's death?"

"Nothing anybody familiar with the case didn't!"

Bancroft had only listened to the interrogation. He just came in and needed it to be smooth and void of logic. But, now, he didn't like Crane's response to his first question.

You better be nice!

He leaned closer. This time, he crashed into the seat beside Detective Hunter.

"We are interested in the specifics, Mr. Crane. What do you know about Thompson's death?" he explained.

"Accident. Thompson drove under the influence and missed the road for a pole!"

"Was he alcoholic?"

"A heavy one. We all knew," he rolled his eyes and swayed his hands in explanation. "I mean, everyone in Dream Farms knew. He couldn't live a day without a bottle!"

"So, nobody ever suggested that someone could have murdered Thompson and gone away, knowing he would be blamed for his bad drinking?"

"None that I knew, then!"

"How about now?"

Crane gradually hated the direction of the interrogation. He couldn't get why the questioning suddenly derailed from him and got centred on Victor Thompson. But he'd also remember that he brought Victor into the picture.

He'd have loved to say "Is this all about Victor now?" but he stood with what won't stir up more questions. "I still know nothing about it."

"He had no family, I guess!"

"None. Not even distant relatives."

Detective Hunter glimmered his eyes around the room and took to his feet. "So, if Victor Thompson was alive, you'd suspected him to be the one planting your DNA on these crime scenes?"

Crane took a deep breath, the weight of Detective Hunter's words hanging heavily in the air. "Victor was always envious of me, jealous of my family and success. We used to be friends, but things turned sour. He blamed me for things that weren't my fault, and sabotaged my work whenever he could."

"And that still doesn't answer the question," Bancroft chipped in.

Crane latched him on a stern gaze and then replied. "Maybe, I do suspect him!"

Detective Hunter's eyes narrowed as he processed the information. He was on his feet now. "Mr Crane, we won't reopen Victor Thompson's case to dig up what might never help this case. Like you said and I can confirm, he died ago. Autopsy said there was an overdose and nothing else could be done. He's a dead man and that could only mean he's not responsible for the DNA implantation."

Grandad nodded, his face etched with a mix of relief and concern. "I understand clearly and that like I've said since I walked in here doesn't change the fact that I know nothing about these victims. I didn't do any of this. You have the wrong man!

Chief Adams Gibson strode in as the interrogation room door swung open, his presence commanding attention. His stern gaze fell upon Crane, and his voice held a note of caution. "He's yet to say something, I guess."

Detective Hunter straightened in his posture from where he stood, his voice steady and resolute. "He knows nothing!"

Chief Adams Gibson is a respected figure in Capeton. Tall. Bulky. Intimidating. For sixteen years, he's been with the Capeton Police Department and only got to the rank of Chief about six years back. He had an eye for details and was known for not deploying mercy or anything compassionate when dealing with suspects in a murder investigation.

His eyes fixed on Crane's face, he waltzed closer, adjusting his well-iron blue service uniform. "You think you will fool my men and fool me too?"

"I'm fooling nobody, Chief. I have no idea how my imprints got to those scenes!" Crane explained.

Chief Adams tapped Crane lightly on the shoulder, signalling him to stand on his feet. He turned around him, their bodies almost colliding. "For close to twenty years in active service, I've seen the alibi of alibi and sadly, yours is way too far from even C-class alibi. You have no other means to explain how your DNA was found in three consecutive crime scenes in the same town you live. Tell me who you work for. Who your partner is. Or why you killed Mr Scot Palmer…"

The tension in the room grew wings and hovered like a cold breeze of a summer night. Crane might never have felt that tense until his arrival. Possibly, the fifty-year-old man had gotten out of excuses. He had no other way to explain to them that he was innocent.

Chief Adam's told him before taking Detective Hunter out of the room. "I'm always available, Mr Crane. Let me know when you're ready to talk."

Crane said nothing. He kept mute.

Stationed at the side of the hallway with Detective Hunter before him, Chief Adam's expression remained stoic, his eyes narrowing as he processed the information. "I've had my suspicions about Crane. His alibis seem too convenient. He may be using his family as a shield. We can't let ourselves be fooled. Keep digging, Hunter. Find the truth, no matter where it leads. Do. Not. Let. This. Catch. Slide."

The gravity of the situation weighed heavily on Bancroft'ss shoulders as he posed the question determining the course of their investigation. It was a question he felt was important to ask even though it had been asked before in a different manner.

"Mr Crane, do you know anyone who might want to implicate you by planting your DNA at these crime scenes?"

Crane looked up, his eyes juddering with confusion. He then lowered his head and lengthened the silence in the room. It was more like he was thinking about it. Bancroft knew how all of these could be hard for him to dissolve. He leaned backwards, giving him some sort of lean privacy.

"Take Victor Thompson out of this. Think wide. You might never get out of this if you don't think critically."

Detective Hunter was back in. Bancroft signaled him and he danced to the tone of the circumstance.

A few seconds later, a flicker of realization crossed Crane's face. Bancroft saw it when he raised his face. He leaned forward, right in Bancroft's direction. His voice was a mix of fear and revelation. "I think I do!"

The room fell into a charged silence, anticipation hanging in the air. Bancroft and Detective Hunter exchanged glances, the puzzle pieces starting to align. Crane's eyes glimmered and he traded glances at both men as they glared at him with a piercing attention.

"Where is he?" Bancroft asked.

Crane nodded in the negative. "They are here with us. In Capeton."

Bancroft turned to Detective Hunter again and then back to Crane.

"Where are they?"

"Dream Farm!"

CHAPTER NINE

JULIUS CAESAR of the Roman Empire once said to his battalion: It is easier to find men who will volunteer to die than to find those willing to endure pain with patience.

Similar patriotism-inducing drills like that became an every day saying for young Bancroft Logan, a seventeen-year-old who finally lived his dream of serving with his nation's Navy.

Years came and passed, yet his dream only kept getting clearer. He fought battles. He learned lessons. He was killed to protect the interest of his country. Until the mission came, it wasn't his first mission off the shores of his country. But, it was his first in the Caribbean. In Cuba. The home of Fidel Castro.

Like in other operations, he knew he would return with his limbs and arms intact. It wasn't a war. It was a covert mission in some rebel-infested zone west of Havana. Highly classified covert operation—the extraction of a high-value target.

The sun hung low in the sky as Lieutenant Junior Grade (LTJG) Bancroft and his team of elite Navy SEALs moved stealthily through the narrow, war-torn streets of West Havana. The scent of smoke and the distant sounds of gunfire lingered in the air, a haunting reminder of the turmoil that plagued the city.

Their mission was clear: neutralize a high-profile target hidden deep within the rebel stronghold and extract him alive. An Iran terrorist with strong bonds with Cuban rebels. Bancroft felt the weight of responsibility settle upon his shoulders as they approached their objective. Every step taken brought them closer to the heart of darkness.

As they turned a corner, the tranquillity shattered like glass. Rebels emerged from the shadows, armed to the teeth, their eyes filled with a fervent desire to protect their cause. Tankers. Humvees. Bazookas. Gunfire erupted, filling the air with a cacophony of deafening blasts and the sharp crack of slender hollow bullets. Black Talon bullets from sophisticated firearms meant for A-Class military units and mercenaries. AR-15s. Barrett M82s. M1 Carbines.

Bancroft moved with calculated precision, his training kicking in as adrenaline surged through his veins. The battle rhythm was fierce and unforgiving, a dance of life and death. The air was thick with the acrid scent of gunpowder as screams of pain mingled with shouts of determination.

He never saw it coming. None of them did. The command centre gave its final greenlight, declaring the coast safe and cold enough to break through. The SEAL Team 6 had the best hands on the radars. Through their sophisticated pre-operational surveillance and reconnaissance, they plough up and mow down a target location, getting favourable enough to notice the tiniest crumb of offset whenever any happens.

Meanwhile, the team is a special mission unit within the Navy SEALs. For years, their primary focus had always been on counterterrorism and hostage rescue operations. The special operations unit didn't make the operation—the commander back at Havana Consulate didn't see it necessary. That was how smooth the ride was mapped out to be.

But, everything went south, leaving Bancroft and the other men at a crossroads they had to fight through with every crumb of energy in them or die.

In the chaos, a grenade exploded, sending shockwaves through the ranks of Bancroft's team. The force of the blast propelled him backwards, his body slamming against a crumbling wall. Pain seared through his senses as shards of debris tore into his flesh. He had always been hit. Slammed. Knocked down by explosions. But not that hard.

His vision blurred, and the world spun in a chaotic whirlwind. The cries of his comrades became distant echoes as darkness enveloped him, dragging him into its abyss. Deep inside, as the pain seared through his bones and began settling on the edge of his spine, he saw himself losing his comrades and the entire fight.

Time slipped away, lost in a void of unconsciousness. And then, with a gasp, Bancroft jolted back to life. It all seemed like the last eternity just passed. His body ached badly, every nerve on edge. The groans of pain and the distant sounds of battle seeped into his consciousness. He was lost in a sea of half-dead corpses gathered in one endless battlefield—some had full bodies that grew too weak to stand while some were reduced to limps, studs and shards of carbon, a ready-made meal for vulture deserts.

Bancroft pushed himself up, the taste of blood on his tongue. His surroundings blurred, his vision obscured by a thick haze of smoke. The remnants of the ambush lay before him—a macabre tableau of fallen comrades and rebel fighters.

His eyes scanned the scene, his heart sinking at the sight of the casualties. Sergeant Rodriguez lay motionless, and his life was extinguished in an instant. Blood pooled beneath him, staining the cracked pavement a deep crimson. The once vibrant spirit of the sergeant had been silenced forever.

Bancroft clenched his jaw, a surge of anger coursing through his veins. He had fought alongside these men, shared laughter and tears, and now they lay broken and lifeless. The horrors of war were etched into his soul, a burden that would forever haunt him.

But as the pain throbbed through his battered body, a realization began to take hold. The battle scars ran deeper than the physical wounds. The memories of countless encounters, of lives cut short and innocence lost, now gripped his mind.

Diagnosed with Post-Traumatic Stress Disorder (PTSD), Bancroft was forced to confront the demons that plagued his mind. The weight of the decision ahead of him pressed upon his weary shoulders. The military had been his life, his purpose, but it had also cost him dearly.

It was time to bid farewell to the military!

He did. After he healed completely from the injuries from the Cuban attack, he gave up the dream. He comforted himself with the belief that he had lived a part of it and would never qualify to be called a coward like some of his commanders would say.

Only cowards look back.

And then, he'd recall the popular quotes from Julius Caesar that were popularized by the most feared commander in the Navy during his time.

It is easier to find men who will volunteer to die than those who are willing to endure pain with patience.

He couldn't erase those words from his subconscious. They made him accept that he fought a good fight despite backing out when needed!

Meanwhile, he had lost his Brazilian lover. Their four-year-old relationship shattered under the weight of his trauma. She could watch him dying every day. He reassured her that he was fine and getting better, but she feared making the wrong decision. She wasn't scared of losing him. She was scared of how she'd be losing him. Perhaps, she was ready to accept any other thing but not the fangs of slow death—so she thought. He was in a coma for weeks.

Back to everyday life, the civilian ways failed him. He expected things to frown at him. Especially at the start. Four months into his new life, he witnessed a failed winery business, and all started to look like he was becoming a symbol of broken dreams.

Still, within the shores of Capeton, he sought solace in a new endeavour. He embraced a role with Midas Securities, delving into the shadows and embracing the life of a private investigator. It was his little way of continuing his military life in a fairly militarized way.

As he reflected on his tumultuous journey, Bancroft was drawn back to that fateful ambush in Havana. The scars of his past collided with the present, fueling his unwavering commitment to uncover the truth. He saw no reason why someone would be after his life, but the memory of that harrowing battle became the catalyst that drove him forward.

In that long reverie, while lost in the warmth of a soft-padded recliner at his apartment's balcony overlooking the rocky hills of Capeton Park, he carried the weight of his past, a constant reminder of the battles fought and the sacrifices made.

The echoes of war reverberated within him, driving his relentless pursuit of justice. Nothing else mattered. PTSD. His job with Midas Securities. His affair with Rachel.

I've come too far to back out!

CHAPTER TEN

BANCROFT LOVED INTERROGATIONS. It was his most enjoyable way of getting leads regardless of how tough the interrogated suspect was.

Two days ago, Otis Crane revealed the names of two individuals he believed might be interested in implicating him in the string of murders, all leading back to his DNA. He pleaded for protection, his eyes filled with fear and desperation.

Detective Christopher Hunter had leaned forward, his voice steady and resolute as he assured Crane of safety. "Crane, we take your safety seriously but need substantial evidence to proceed. If your leads prove valid, we will ensure your protection."

Crane nodded, understanding the gravity of the situation. He had taken a deep breath, his gaze fixed on the detectives before letting out the name slowly like it was some landmine that had to be installed carefully.

The first person he mentioned was Finnegan George. The man, who was later figured out to have a Scottish origin, is the Head of Forestry at Dream Farms, the same company Crane works as a lumberman. Crane suspected Finnegan George to possibly be after him because he had on several occasions refused to be a part of the wood supply fraud he was running in the Supply Unit of the company.

"I'm in charge of the timber. I know how many logs we fall weekly and how my team sizes. He knows we're aware of the dubiousness. All of us are at the lumbering unit. But, he knows the authorities will only listen to me."

Bancroft didn't have to tell Crane to the face, but he felt it was enough reason for the man to want him dead and gone at all costs.

Detective Hunter had exchanged a glance with Bancroft as the weight of the accusation sank in. He imagined Finnegan George, a man in a position of power, potentially using his authority to orchestrate fraudulent acts and attempting to frame innocent people as a cover-up. The possibility sent a shiver down their spine. He wondered what more and how deep the corruption might run.

Bancroft remembered asking Crane if he had any piece of evidence that could support his claim and tie Finnegan George to these crimes.

Crane gave them hope but there was more. The second person.

He had swallowed hard with his fingers fidgeting nervously when he said the name.

"Jeff Griffin!"

"He's an investment banker who visits Capeton on weekends. He believes I killed his sister, my ex-wife. We've been at odds for years, and he may have a vendetta against me."

"Your wife's dead?" Detective Hunter chipped in, his face etched with surprise.

Crane nodded. "Lucy's not Daniel's mother. She's my second. I lost my happiness a long time ago. But my kids needed a mother. I got them, Lucy!"

The room breathed with silence and the two men allowed the discovery to sink it.

"Did you?" Bancroft asked. He wasn't sure it was a good question, considering the clear signs that Crane had just been reminded of a pain he's been struggling to put aside.

"Did I do what?"

"Kill her!" Bancroft completed. He didn't want to. It sounded more odd than he ever wanted it to sound. But, at the same time, he didn't want to leave the question hanging.

"She died of cancer. Breast cancer!"

Bancroft had raised an eyebrow, intrigued by Crane's struggles. He began seeing reasons and coalescing the dots as to why Crane looked weaker than his strength. He equally saw the possibility of extreme animosity between Crane and Jeff Griffin.

The intertwining webs of personal vendettas and the potential for revenge made for a compelling motive. But as an investigator who rarely put his eggs in a basket, Bancroft felt they couldn't and shouldn't solely rely on personal disputes to conclude.

The entire conversation came alive.

"Crane, it's crucial to establish a solid connection between Jeff Griffin and the crimes," Bancroft stated, his tone measured. "We'll delve into his background and investigate any leads that could shed light on his involvement."

Crane nodded, his eyes glimmering with a glimmer of hope. "Thank you, Bancroft. I know it's a long shot, but I had to share these suspicions. My life depends on finding the truth."

Detective Hunter leaned forward. He had to reecho his promise to protect himself and his family. "Crane, we'll do everything possible to ensure your safety and your family."

Bancroft had long waited for Detective Hunter to add the clause but didn't. He did it himself. "Crane," he called out softly when he was about to be led back into custody until things began to take shape.

"I'm afraid freedom will be a fairytale to you if any of all you've said is false. We don't harbour dishonest people."

Though harbouring doubts about the validity of the leads, Bancroft understood the necessity of exploring every possible angle. He saw every reason to believe that these men could be after Crane but couldn't fall facedown for it.

With their sights set on Finnegan George and Jeff Griffin, Bancroft and Detective Hunter embarked on the next phase of the investigation.

As they pursued justice for Crane and sought to unravel the mysteries that haunted the Capeton, they knew the path ahead would be treacherous.

Crane was no free man just yet.
He was denied bail and left in the custody of Capeton PD. It was both for his safety and that of the investigation.

CHAPTER ELEVEN

BANCROFT AND DETECTIVE HUNTER stepped out of their car, their breaths forming plumes in the chilly night air. A few more minutes later, their footsteps echoed on the path leading to Jeff Griffin's stately residence, the Craneur of the mansion casting a sombre shadow over their mission.

Detective Hunter glanced at Logan, a shared understanding passing between them. They had braved countless crime scenes and interrogations, but the complexities of this case and the delicate nature of their suspect made this encounter all the more significant. The truth they sought lay shrouded within the corridors of secrets and emotions.

With a firm resolve, they approached the elaborately carved front door, the weight of their badges resting heavily on their chests. The door creaked open, revealing the polished interior of Griffin's home—a testament to wealth and privilege. The aroma of fine leather and freshly cut flowers permeated the air, creating an ambience of cultivated elegance.

They were ushered into the study by some bulky bodyguard, where Griffin awaited their arrival. The room exuded an air of muted sophistication, its rich mahogany furnishings and soft lighting lending an air of intimacy. The walls were adorned with intricate paintings and family portraits, all carrying a lifetime of memories and hidden narratives.

Griffin's piercing gaze met theirs as they settled into their seats. His eyes betrayed a mix of weariness and wonder as if he had long grappled with the demons of his past. The silence stretched, each man sizing up the other, the unspoken tension weighing heavily upon them.

Detective Hunter took a deep breath, breaking the stillness. "Mr. Griffin, we appreciate your cooperation in this investigation. We understand that your connection to Otis Crane has added a layer of complexity to the case."

Griffin nodded, his features a mask of stoicism. "I want justice to prevail, Detective Hunter. My sister's memory deserves nothing less."

Not like anybody deserves less!

Bancroft leaned forward, his gaze steady. "We are here to uncover the truth, Mr. Griffin. We believe that Otis Crane's DNA was found at the crime scene. All three of them. Can you provide insights into how his genetic material might have ended there?"

Griffin's brow furrowed momentarily, a flicker of confusion crossing his face. He composed himself, a steely resolve settling in his eyes. "Detectives, I assure you that I do not know Otis' DNA being present at the crime scene. Such a claim is unfathomable to me. He should be in a position to answer that. I can only speak to the resentment that developed between us over time."

Detective Hunter leaned back, his eyes scanning the room, taking in the paintings and portraits that adorned the walls. They spoke of family bonds, love, and loss—echoes of the past, the untold stories that may hold the key to the truth they sought.

He shifted his focus back to Griffin, his voice measured. "Mr Griffin, we understand the complicated dynamics between you and Otis Crane. Your sister's passing undoubtedly had a profound impact on your relationship. Could it be that your emotions, your resentment towards Otis, clouded your judgment or led you to take matters into your own hands?"

Griffin's eyes flared with a mix of frustration and, again, curiosity. "Detectives, I loved my sister deeply, and her death devastated me. But I would never resort to violence or tampering with evidence. I have been grieving, seeking closure and justice for her."

Detective Hunter studied Griffin, his intuition guiding him as he searched for the truth hidden within the layers of emotion within the silence between his words and the meat of his eyeballs. "Mr Griffin, we understand the complexities of familial bonds. Sometimes, the weight of loss can blur the lines between justice and personal vendetta. We implore you to be honest with us, as the truth is our ultimate objective."

Griffin's jaw tightened, his gaze unwavering. "I have no reason to lie, Detective Hunter. I want justice, not revenge. I believe in the process and the truth that will prevail."

The room fell into a heavy silence, the detectives and Griffin locked in a battle of words and perceptions. The investigation stretched out before them. It was something close to a dead-end.

As Detective Hunter slightly relented, Bancroft continued the interrogation, his questions probed deeper, chipping away at the façade Griffin had carefully constructed. The room's atmosphere grew charged with the weight of truth and deception mingling.

Many minutes came and passed, the pendulum of the interrogation swinging back and forth, the detectives skillfully navigating the intricate dance between truth and lies. Each word spoken, each emotion laid bare, brought them closer to the elusive truth that awaited them.

There was yet no visible trace of a lie!

The study's walls stood as silent witnesses, the paintings and portraits reflecting the turmoil and

hidden desires beneath the surface. Bancroft and Detective Hunter
 remained resolute.

As the night wore on, the intensity of the interrogation grew, the boundaries between right and wrong, truth and falsehood, blurring. Griffin's demeanour shifted, revealing cracks in his carefully constructed armour.

Only time would tell if justice would prevail if the intricacies of this case would be untangled, and if the truth would finally be brought to light.

For now. Mr Griffin held nothing.

The truth existed but certainly not within the walls of that mansion.

CHAPTER TWELVE

IT WAS THE PERFECT TIME TO GRAB a cup of cappuccino. The scorching heat of the afternoon sun beat down on Capeton, making the air feel heavy and stifling. Bancroft sought refuge from the oppressive weather in a cosy cafe, seeking solace in the comforting aroma of freshly brewed coffee.

As he settled into a corner table, the steam rising from his cup of hot coffee, Bancroft allowed himself a moment of respite. His mind buzzed with the ongoing investigation, the puzzle pieces slowly coming together. It was the best time of the day to take time off and reflect. But amidst the chaos, his attention was drawn to a familiar face in the distance.

He saw her through the see-through glass walls of the cafe.

The woman was a figure of intrigue to him. He didn't have to lose her. He dropped dollar bills on the table and headed for the door, his eyes toward the woman.

The closer he was to the door, the clearer her picture became. She was the one. He couldn't ever mistake her for somebody. It was Detective Elaine Murphy. She had gone completely out of sight after Detective Hunter confronted her.

Keeping a distance as he trailed behind, Bancroft watched as she squeezed her frame into a jalopy that screeched beside her.

It wasn't a cab. It wasn't her car. Who then was it?

As a law enforcement officer, and perhaps, one who could be hiding something, Elaine was always alerted. Bancroft could tell from how thoroughly she scanned the crowd before entering the car. However, he could take a bullet to prove she didn't see him.

She didn't have to!

He hopped on the next cab and followed them. He had no idea what the chase could hold. But he sure knew that he'd never get his hands on anything if he didn't keep following.

The trail ended at an apartment on Silicon Boulevard. Bancroft dropped from a distance and made it to the apartment on foot. It was a huge one, about six stories, one of the tallest buildings in Capeton.

Bancroft felt angry when he made it to the garage where she sleekly walked in but found no one. He kept cranking until a parked GMC truck drove out of its parking spot. From beneath the truck, he sighted four legs. He was sure a pair of those were Elaine's.

Out of the blues came another car that got him lying flat on the coal-tarred garage ground. He wasn't seen but he knew he had missed a lot. Alas. He saw him. The man who drove the truck. Tiny but plumpy and blonde. He wore a faded black t-shirt and had brown hair that doubled his ugliness.

Bancroft saw the other driver from the car that Nuts drove in. He looked like a club bodyguard. Tall like a high-rise. Built like a brick house. Intimidating as a jaguar. The truck driver handed Detective Elaine a box and the bodyguard-like driver opened the door for her.
The truck driver bowed to the car when the engine came alive. Detective Elaine secured her escape but Bancroft knew he at least had something to feed his

curiosity with. The man didn't look like a match to him. He was way too weak to assume a defence.

Sensing a movement around him, the man turned towards the truck door only to drive his face into Bancroft's hard kick.

"Were you heading somewhere?" Bancroft shrieked, waltzing towards him as he struggled to hoist his frame. With more kicks, he sprawled to the floor, grunting and gasping for breath.

A flurry of punches rented the air as Bancroft engaged in a fierce struggle chokehold. "You better start talking. Will you?"

The garage echoed with grunts and the thud of hard punches. Bancroft was in charge. He dodged and trapped the weak retaliatory jabs from the man. He must have spent more time at the pub than breathing oxygen.

With every blow to his potbelly, the man's resistance grew weaker, his face a mask of pain and desperation. Bancroft saw his opening and seized the moment, delivering a final blow that sent the man crashing to the floor. This time, he was ready to talk. As his body crumbled in defeat, he saw no need to keep getting humiliated.

Bancroft wasted no time, his heart pounding with adrenaline and purpose. He swiftly produced a pair of handcuffs, his hands steady despite the chaos surrounding them. The metal clanged against the man's wrists as he was secured, the weight of his actions finally catching up to him.

"Who the fuck are you?" Bancroft growled, his voice laced with authority and angst.

"Ah…ah nnn. I-I…" the man stammered, struggling to breathe as Bancroft brushed his fat face against the top of the truck.

"Who are you?" Bancroft hollered again, giving him space to breathe.

"D-Da-Davies. Davies Webber. Uber driver."

Bancroft whacked him with more blows and he smacked him against the truck again. He pulled his Glock and cocked it.

"One more lie. I'll fix your brain!"

"Pl-please. I ain't lying. I've got an ID in the glove compartment."

Bancroft leaned backwards, pointing the gun right at the back of his head. He unlocked the cuffs, opened the door and nodded inside. "Get it!"

He handcuffed him, leaned against the truck and looked through the ID.

Davies B. Webb. Uber Driver.

"Who's she?"

"I swear I-I have no idea!"

"You think I'm fucking with you?" Bancroft yelled, hitting him hard.

"Come on! I swear. I had an order around Maryland Avenue. Some guy phoned and claimed the order. He had a different phone line. I think it's unlisted. He made me pick up a waybill at Clifford Boulevard.

Clifford Boulevard.

The name of the street rang a bell. It was the same street where Otis Crane lived.

"Who delivered the waybill?"

"Some black guy in a blue uniform."

"Stop messing around with me! What the hell was the name of the courier agency."

"Oh. That? MegEx. The one with the tall building in Central Capeton."

Bancroft turned around to monitor the garage. He sort of heard an incoming vehicle but it suddenly watered down. It never came. Maybe, he's hallucinating again.

"What was it?" he asked Davies again.

"The what?"

Why the hell is he so dumb?

"The waybill item!"

"A box. Some mystery box."

"What was in it?"

"No. No opening. No checking. Rule number one. Code of conduct. I didn't touch it!"

Bancroft hit him hard again. "You didn't touch what?" he groaned.

"Okay. Okay. I did touch it but I didn't open it."
"You got an unwrapped box on a ride with no one with it and you didn't open it?"

"I-I did not. It's against our work ethic."

"The guy on the phone. He told you to bring it here. Didn't he?"

"Yes. That's someone coming to get it!"

"How long have you been here?"

"Roughly 45 minutes!"

Bancroft loosened his grip on Davies. Probably, the terrified Davies felt that was it. It wasn't. Bancroft still had more troubles for him. Swiftly, he spun him around, pulled out the cartridge from his gun, shovelled it in the air as if for Davies to admire and then put it back. He cocked the gun and released it right into the truck's blinker.

Davies shuddered in terror as his eyes dilated in awe. His lips twitched and his limbs grew watery as he watched shards of glass from the broken blinker clattered to the ground in different directions. He first thought of how to escape being shot and then he'd fix the blinker without getting grounded by his no-nonsense Manager.

"Do you know her?" Bancroft asked, this time, his tone soft but firm.

"I do not know her...I swear I-I don't!"

Bancroft stepped forward, shutting the door of the truck.

"The box...did you open it? I won't ask you this again!"

Davies kept mute, his entire frame jerky-trembling like one being electrocuted. He was electrocuted but not by electrons by the adrenaline breezing surge without his veins due to the gun pointed at his forehead.

"I-I…"

"Spare me the god-damned stammer…" Bancroft blew another shot. This time, it found the ground beside the truck's tire.

"Yes…yes…yes. I-I opened the box!"

"I see," Bancroft lowered his gun and spun him around again, making him face the truck.

"What was it?"

"A paper."

"What do you mean by paper?"

"Some sort of a special paper!"

"Some sort of special paper!" Bancroft mimicked him and steered his hand to the windshield of the truck. "How about that?" he nodded.

"No. No map. It was a map."

"What map?"

"A map to a building. It was an enlarged plan of the building."

"How do you know that?"

"I-I'm an architect by profession. It was a blueprint for the underground sewage system to the building. I saw signs of a tunnel network. They were unlabeled."

Bancroft sheathed his gun. "What do you think it is for?"

"I can't say."

Bancroft thought for a while, swirling around as if raiding the garage for any sign of an intrusion. Davies was fully alert too. His pulse must have slowed down but his eyes never left the damaged blinker.

Bancroft turned to him. "Get in the truck!"

Davies' eyes splayed widely. "You've got to book a ride. I'm being watched. They'd think you're paying me for the ride," he narrated, countering the order.

"Get in the truck, Davies. It's not a request!"

"But…"

"Get in the fucking truck," Bancroft yelled, pulling his gun again.

When Bancroft stopped him and nodded across, Davies was about to get into the driver seat. "Passenger's seat!"

"You wanna dri…"

"You talk too much and you know what I do to people like you? I shut them up my way!"

Davies entered the truck, his mouth still ready to spill more questions.

Inside the truck, Bancroft turned to Davies, slumped into the passenger's seat, and kept staring.

It was more like the gun in Bancroft's hand was a latent sellotape placed across his lips.

"Where's the damn tracker?" he asked Davies.

"Right above you," he nodded to the rearview mirror. "They see my every move and would demand a charge for every drop of gas I used to cover it?"

Bancroft reached out to the device. He studied briefly. It had a green beeping light. Davies couldn't help but pull a whimper when Bancroft switched off the tracker.

"No. No. They're going to send the cops after me! That's a breach!"

Ignoring him like he didn't exist, Bancroft turned out the ignition and switched the gear to reverse, peering backwards for an incoming car. He had assumed a perfect drive position at the drop of a hat and then turned his gun to the confused Davies.

"Where's the building?"

Davies kept mute. He only talked when Bancroft lowered the gun's tip right towards his midsection below his belt.

"127 Crestwood Avenue."

Bancroft was taken aback.

"There's nowhere like that in Capeton.

"Not here!"

"Where?"

"Montebello"

CHAPTER THIRTEEN

THE MOON CAST A glow upon the deserted streets of Montebello, its pale light flickering through the slivers of darkness. Bancroft hadn't been there for a long time.

Montebello is more developed than Capeton. That made it an abode of things that couldn't survive in Capeton. Street race. Free flow of illicit drugs and nightlife not moved by anybody.

Unlike Capeton, with just a Police Department, Montebello runs a Police Department and a Sheriff's Department. Yet, crimes in the twin waxed stronger. It was a place for people like Bancroft, who loved being challenged to find steady cases.

Bancroft had a handful of reasons to move to Montebello or remain in Capeton but convinced Midas Securities to open a franchise in North Montebello but he eventually saw no need for that!

He loved Capeton. He grew up there. And in a way, had memoires he'd never loved to live behind.

Serving in the Navy had taken him away from the twin enough, He needed to have more time at home and build all his count.

In the confines of a parked truck, Bancroft sat in silence, his sharp eyes fixed on the figure before him— Davies Webber. Beads of perspiration adorned Davies' forehead, betraying his nervous disposition as they waited in the shadows. Bancroft passed Davies a packet of gum. "You might need this!" he said.

The air hung heavy with anticipation, thickening the atmosphere with a veil of mystery and intrigue.

"So, Davies," Bancroft spoke, his voice a low, steady rumble, "you sure this is the place? Right?"

Davies' gaze met Bancroft's unwaveringly in the rearview mirror, his hands gripping the steering wheel. Bancroft had uncuffed him and let him take the wheel along the way. It was the only way he could look out for a possible invasion.

"I didn't mean to get caught up in this mess, Mr. Bancroft. I was just taking an order, minding my own business. You know, when I stumbled upon all of these!"

Bancroft leaned forward, his piercing eyes locked on Davies' reflection. "I believe you. Come on!"

The engine roared to life, breaking the silence as the truck merged into the dimly lit streets of Crestwood Avenue. Davies' hands trembled on the steering wheel, mirroring the visible tension in the air. Shadows danced across the buildings, concealing secrets and untold truths that awaited their discovery.

Bancroft's senses sharpened as the truck navigated the almost empty streets, every nerve attuned to the impending search for answers. The anticipation pulsed within him, heightening his awareness of the mysteries ahead. The enigma of the warehouse loomed before them, a puzzle waiting to be solved.

Finally, they arrived at their destination—an unassuming warehouse nestled amidst the shadows. Its worn facade whispered of concealed secrets and concealed activities. The air grew heavy with intrigue as Bancroft and Davies stepped out of the truck, their footsteps echoing through the silence of the night.

"We are here. I guess!" Bancroft exclaimed before Davies put out the engine.

Together, they approached the warehouse, its imposing doors as guardians of the enigma within. But before then, Bancroft has held Davies against the truck again. "You better not be joking with me!"

As the little ruffle died out, Bancroft glanced at Davies, their eyes meeting, silently acknowledging the risks and uncertainties ahead. The stakes had been raised, the journey fraught with danger, but neither man wavered in their pursuit of the truth.

Slowly, Bancroft patted him on the shoulder as they waltzed ahead like an ops unit on a stealth mission in some military installation somewhere in Asia.

With each step they took, the warehouse grew larger, its presence more imposing. The air crackled with tension as they crossed the threshold, venturing into the belly of the unknown. Their footsteps echoed through the cavernous space, the sound swallowed by the vastness that surrounded them.

Is it always this empty?

As they explored the warehouse, their senses heightened, attuned to every sound, every flicker of movement. The suspense built, thickening the air with anticipation. They examined crates and boxes, their fingers tracing invisible paths of discovery. Yet, despite their meticulous search, the evidence they sought remained elusive, veiled within the depths of the warehouse.

Bancroft turned to Davies, and his whispers fledged with determination. "Keep searching, Davies."

Davies nodded, his eyes reflecting fear and crawling bravery. Together, they pressed on, their exploration becoming a dance of intrigue and perseverance. Shadows shifted, playing tricks on their perception, hinting at concealed truths that slipped through their fingers.

Almost an hour passed, yet the warehouse yielded no tangible answers. Pursuing truth became a game of patience. Their resolve was tested at every turn. But Bancroft and Davies remained undeterred, driven by a shared determination to uncover the dormant secrets within the warehouse's walls.

"This must be some abandoned factory," Davies said, his heart studding as they moved deeper into the warehouse.

Davies' voice seemed to jerk up a movement. It was heard from the tiny cubicle not from their left. Bancroft signalled Davies to only stay behind while he took the lead. Slow but steady, they closed in on the cubicle. It looked like its enclosed, like the type in hospitals, made of perforated boards and high-quality wood.

The closer they got. The more the cracking sound increased in intensity. With a nod, Davies stepped aside and Bancroft knocked down the cubicle's door at the expense of a kick. Davies' scream rented the air and lingered like the remnants of a staccato. A black cat leapt out of the cubicle and almost landed on his face. The terror almost knocked the air out of him. He didn't see it coming. Plus, he hates cats.

"That was so close!" Bancroft exclaimed, trying not to laugh even though he had every reason to.

As they continued their search, the darkness enshrouding the warehouse seemed to thicken, mirroring the uncertainty that loomed over their investigation.

Bancroft had no flicker of hope that they'd ever find something within the warehouse. He signalled Davies and they pulled back. As a private investigator with many years of searching warehouses and tearing through apartments, Bancroft knew that not every search comes off with something to hold onto.

He admitted that the search wasn't just fruitless but held a meaning. Detective Elaine must have noticed his alertness towards her and had him drive from Capeton to Montebello to search an empty warehouse.

At the same time, Bancroft considered something quite unfamiliar but could be true.
Is she buying time?
Or distracting me!

CHAPTER FOURTEEN

THE EARLY MORNING SUN filtered through the curtains, casting a soft glow upon the room as Rachel and Bancroft engaged in another heated argument. The tension crackled in the air, their voices filled with frustration and despair. It seemed as though their relationship was slowly unravelling, held together by fraying threads.

As their voices rose in intensity, the shrill ring of the landline pierced through the chaos. Bancroft's heart skipped a beat, the terror in his eyes impossible to hide from Rachel. His hand trembled as he reached for the phone, unsure who it was and what it was about.

It was the Chief. Adams Gibson. He hadn't called him directly in a long time.

He said he needed him at Blinkton Train Station. He sounded low but firm and even if he broke no usual news, Bancroft felt an inkling that all wasn't well. Getting a call from the Chief himself indicated a big red light.

Another life lost?

A second murder?

Of all the places, he wondered why the Chief would see him in the train station lounge. A place of bustling commuters and daily routines, quite unsafe to discuss the details of a murder investigation. The gravity of the situation and whatever it'd be settled upon Bancroft, his mind swirling with the dark possibilities that awaited him.

He was about to phone Detective Hunter when Rachel's cough jerked his attention.

"It's just 7:00 am, Bancroft. The PDs phoned you on a Saturday morning. Are you now a cop and I do not know about it, Bancroft?"

Bancroft shrugged and moved aside. "Who becomes a cop overnight?" he defended.
"It is only a cop that another partner calls by 7:00 am on a Saturday."

Turning to Rachel, his voice strained with urgency, and he revealed the truth. "It's not Detective Hunter. It's the Chief."

"Adam's Gibson?"

Bancroft nodded as he made for the wardrobe.

"What does he want?"

"Nothing that I'm so sure of just yet. It sounded like some sort of emergency. The Chief only calls when it's necessary!"

Rachel's eyes widened, a mix of fear and frustration across her face. She looked at Bancroft, pleading with him to understand. "So, you're leaving. Aren't you?"

"What else am I supposed to do, Rachel? He wants me there?" Bancroft barked, unbuttoning the shirt he had just pulled down from the wardrobe.
"You're not answerable to him. You're just a private investigator for crying out loud. He's got an entire Police Department to himself. Why you?"

"For years, I've worked hand in hand with Capeton PD. I might not be answerable to the Chief but his immense support to my investigations and his belief in me makes me loyal to him!"

"You don't have to!"

"You won't understand this, Rachel. I have to run!"

"Do I even mean anything to you, Bancroft?" she asked, a silent sob buried in her voice. Bancroft could feel it but it didn't matter to him. Only the meeting with the Chief did.

"Rachel," he'd call her so subtly as he emptied the cup of coffee he abandoned on the table. "Sometimes, life won't let us do the things we'd love to do. You mean a lot to me but before me is what's worth my time more than any other thing."

"But what about us, Bancroft? What about our relationship? This case is tearing us apart. You have to choose — me or this relentless pursuit of justice."

Bancroft's heart heaved when the words got to him. He felt torn between his unwavering commitment to the case and the woman he loved. He reached out, and his voice filled with desperation this time. "Rachel, you have to understand. This is bigger than us. I can't turn my back on the truth, on the lives that are in danger."

"Even if it means turning your back on me?"

"I'm not turning my back on you!"

"It seems like you are to me and of course, every sensible person out there will admit the same," she retorted.

Bancroft leaned closer, his teeth bared and fists clenched into a tight ball. "Make of this whatever it is you wish. But this is a fight I won't back out of!"

A tear slipped down Rachel's cheek as she drew a shaky breath. "I can't keep living in this constant state of fear and uncertainty…of complete neglect. It's over, Bancroft. I can't bear the weight of your obsession any longer."

The words landed like a heavy blow, their finality hanging in the air. Bancroft stood frozen, his heart shattering into a million pieces. The realization of his sacrifices and the toll his pursuit of justice had taken on his personal life crashed down upon him with unforgiving force.

Silence enveloped the room, broken only by the distant sirens echoing from a distance. The world outside carried on, indifferent to the pain that consumed them. Bancroft knew that he had to make a choice that would shape the course of his life and the lives of those around him.

With a heavy heart, Bancroft nodded, his voice laced with sorrow. "I understand, Rachel. I'm sorry for everything." The weight of his words hung in the air, a poignant acknowledgement of the fractures that had formed between them.

As Rachel gathered herself and made her way to the door of their room, completely oblivious to Bancroft, a profound sense of loss settled upon Bancroft. The woman he loved, his anchor in the storm, was slipping away. But he couldn't let grief consume him, not when Capeton cried out for justice.

"See you, Bancroft," she rifled out, a satchel hung across her shoulder. Her scent sparked memories as she hurried past Bancroft, heading for the door.

"Wait," he grabbed her arm but she broke out of his grip with a strength Bancroft never saw coming.

"Don't touch me, you monster!"

As the door closed behind Rachel, Bancroft took a deep breath, his resolve strengthening. Just as he began to gather his thoughts, the phone's ringing shattered the silence. His heart skipped a beat, sending a chill down his spine.

Bancroft rushed to answer the call, his voice trembling with anticipation.
It's Detective Hunter.

On the other end of the line, his voice erupted in hushed tones, delivering news that would thrust Bancroft deeper into the darkness that consumed Capeton.

"There's been another murder."

"When?"

"This morning!"

The words hung in the air, a chilling reminder of the relentless nature of the crimes unfolding in the Capeton. Bancroft felt a surge of adrenaline coursing through his veins, his senses heightened. The investigation demanded his unwavering attention, pulling him deeper into the web of mystery and danger.

As he swung his gaze to the door, Bancroft knew there was no turning back. Rachel was out of his picture. The choice had been made, and the path ahead was treacherous, back to Detective Hunter who was still around despite Bancroft's poor concentration on the phone.

"Where?

"Blinkton!"

CHAPTER FIFTEEN

THE MURDER SCENE WAS enveloped in an eerie silence as Detective Bancroft arrived, his mind still filled with the lingering echoes of his recent struggle with Rachel. Beside him was Detective Hunter, a loyal partner who had been with Bancroft through thick and thin. The air hung heavy with the scent of fear and uncertainty as they approached the scene, where the medic and forensic team were already wrapping up their procedures.

Bancroft took a moment to survey the area, his eyes tracing the contours of the crime scene like an artist studying a masterpiece. The dim light of the setting sun cast long shadows across the pavement, amplifying the sense of mystery that clung to the air. The victim, Graeme George, lay motionless on the ground, his young life extinguished too soon. The sight sent a shiver down Bancroft's spine, a stark reminder of the darkness that lurked within humanity.

As Bancroft began to gather information, he sought out the station guards and other witnesses who had been present during the initial moments of the crime. Each conversation felt like a step back in time, a momentary glimpse into the past. The witnesses' words echoed in his mind, their voices tainted with sorrow and trepidation.

One witness, an elderly man with weathered features, recounted seeing a shadowy figure lurking in the vicinity just before the incident occurred. The man's voice quivered as he recalled the fear that gripped him, leaving a lasting impression on his senses. "I tell ya, detective, I've never seen anything like it. The way that person moved, it sent chills down my spine. Quick as a fox, they were."

They?

Another witness, a young woman with tear-streaked cheeks, spoke of the chaos that erupted when the news of Graeme's murder spread through the train station. "People were screaming, crying. It was like a nightmare come to life. I couldn't believe it when I heard what happened to poor Graeme. He was such a bright young soul."

Bancroft listened intently to each account, his mind piecing together the fragments of information like a jigsaw puzzle. But as he delved deeper, he sensed a disquieting truth lurking beneath the surface. Something was amiss, something that didn't quite add up.

His gaze turned towards the station guard, a middle-aged man with weary eyes who had been stationed at the entrance. "Tell me, were there any other officers here before us?" Bancroft asked, his voice laced with a touch of suspicion.

The guard shifted uneasily as if wrestling with a hidden secret. After a moment's hesitation, he finally spoke. "I can't say. I just resumed my shift. You might ask someone who has been here all along."

Bancroft kept studying the scene in detail. The buzz. The tears. The sorrow. The pain. A voice jolted his attention.

"Bancroft Logan," I guess, the feminine figure answered. Flashing an ID. "Amy Borak. Head of security. Blinkton Train Station!"

"Heard so much about what you do for the station! The Police still need some winning people."

"It's sad it's happening on a bad day. Right under my nose," Amy began explaining.

"What do you have on the ground?"

"Our cameras couldn't do a clean job. It must have been quite taxing to get clear footage from that distance."

"Nothing to hold from the pre-murder footage?"

"None that can be meaningful."

"Did any cop hit here before us!"

"I heard some rumours but I saw her myself."

Bancroft surrendered his comfort, comparing the possibility to his dream.

"A female cop, if memory serves me right.

"Wore a grey sweatshirt?" He asked. She had on a black leather jacket."

Bancroft's eyebrows furrowed in confusion. The revelation sent a ripple of unease through him. Why had no one mentioned this earlier? What was the significance of this mysterious female officer?

With more questions than answers, Bancroft knew he had only scratched the surface of a much larger conspiracy. The puzzle pieces were falling into place, but the picture they formed remained elusive, obscured by shadows and half-truths.

Closing his eyes, Bancroft took a deep breath, inhaling the essence of the crime scene. It was a symphony of senses—the sight of Graeme's lifeless body, the lingering smell of death, the touch of an invisible presence. The chapter had just begun, but the story was far from over.

Find Elaine!

CHAPTER SIXTEEN

THERE WAS NO DNA PRINT of Otis Crane this time. The absence of any fingerprints around the lifeless body of Graeme George sent a chilling realization coursing through Detective Bancroft. It shattered the remnants of hope he had been holding onto, leaving him grappling with a sense of desolation that threatened to engulf him.

Could it mean Crane was innocent all along? Or. Did he only exhaust his role in the entire game?

In the dimly lit interrogation room, Detective Bancroft sat across from Finnegan George, the grieving father who firmly believed his family was being targeted. The weight of tragedy hung heavy in the air, casting a sombre atmosphere over the room. Bancroft fixed his gaze upon George, studying every flicker of emotion across his face.

Leaning forward, Bancroft carefully chose his words, his voice a blend of determination and suspicion. "Mr George, I understand the pain you're going through, but I need to address a matter that has come to our attention. There are indications of a potential connection between the recent supply fraud in the Forestry Department of Dream Farms and your position as its head. Can you shed any light on this matter?"

George's eyes widened in genuine surprise, his features contorting with disbelief. He leaned back in his chair, his voice laced with genuine concern as he kept staring at Bancroft.

"I thought this was about my dead son?" he queried.

"What else do you think it is?"

Ignoring Bancroft's question. "Detective, I can assure you that I have no knowledge of supply fraud within my department. I have worked tirelessly to uphold the company's integrity and protect its interests."

Bancroft maintained a steady gaze, his eyes probing for any cracks in George's composure. The burden of suspicion hung heavily between them, each passing moment weighed down by the gravity of the situation. With a careful motion, Bancroft reached into his briefcase and retrieved a pair of documents—the original supply document and the forged one.

Placing the documents on the table between them, Bancroft raised an eyebrow. "Mr George, these documents tell a different story. One is an authentic supply document, while the other is a forgery. The disparity raises questions about the operations within your department. Can you explain this discrepancy?"

George's face paled as his gaze darted between the two documents. His voice wavered, betraying a mix of uncertainty and desperation. "Detective, I... I can't explain how this happened. I swear to you I had no involvement in any fraudulent practices. My dedication to the company and its employees has always been unwavering."

Detective Hunter, observing the exchange from the side, interjected with a measured tone. "Mr George, I understand the weight of the situation you find yourself in. However, finding your son's murderer remains our top priority."

George raised his brows, trading glances between Bancroft and Detective Hunger.

"With due evidence, we will thoroughly investigate the matter of the supply fraud in due time," Detective Hunter added.

A flicker of relief crossed George's face, and gratitude mingled with lingering worry. He realized that, for the moment, the immediate focus was on bringing justice for his son rather than delving into potential corporate misconduct.

As the weight of suspicion lifted momentarily, Detective Bancroft couldn't shake the nagging feeling that someone else had arrived at the crime scene before him—Detective Elaine Murphy. Her expertise and insights could hold valuable information that might illuminate the shadows enveloping Graeme George's murder. But now is not the time to pursue that avenue.

Bancroft decided to push the interrogation further, seeking to understand George's perspective on the connection between the fraud and his son's death. "Mr George, given your position in the Forestry Department, do you believe there could be any correlation between the fraudulent activities and the tragedy that befell your son?"

George's brows furrowed, his face contorting with genuine confusion. "Detective, I honestly don't know. I can't fathom how my son's murder could be connected to fraudulent practices. It's a distressing thought, but I don't have any information suggesting such a link."

Bancroft nodded, understanding George's position. The web of secrets seemed to grow more intricate with every passing moment, entangling the lives of the innocent in a tapestry of darkness.

Bancroft left the room with a heavy heart as the interrogation ended, knowing that tangible answers might elude him for now. He needed a fresh perspective, someone who had witnessed the crime scene with a different lens.

At that moment, his thoughts drifted back to Detective Elaine Murphy. Her arrival at the scene before he held a wealth of untapped information. The memory of her enigmatic words echoed in his mind.

Every dog has its day.

Bancroft knew he needed to seek her out to uncover the truths she might have gleaned from that crucial first encounter.

It is her day!

CHAPTER SEVENTEEN

DESPITE THE TOUGHNESS of the case, Bancroft hadn't completely given up on Rachel. The weight of their connection compelled him to seek her out, to remind her of what they shared and how crucial this case was to his career as a private investigator. That night, driven by determination, he headed to the club where Rachel worked undercover as a stripper.

"You sure this is a great idea?" Detective Hunter had asked Bancroft back in the car when he mentioned that he intended to speak with Detective Elaine.

"She's all shades of suspicion. I know that. She smells of that. But we can't miss chances. She got to the crime scene before we did. She might know what we don't!"

"Ever wondered how she always arrives before we do?"

"Not particularly," Bancroft chipped in, tightening his grip on the steers as he sighed at a reversing truck ahead of them.

They were at the club!

As Bancroft pushed open the entrance door after passing the heavily-built bouncers, the pulsating music pounded through his chest, mingling with the swirling haze of cigarette smoke.

The air was thick with anticipation, and the atmosphere charged with raw energy. Bancroft's eyes scanned the crowd, searching for someone. Rachel's familiar face amidst the sea of bodies gyrating to the beat.

And then, there she was, a vision of seductive grace, captivating the audience with every move. His heart swelled with a mix of longing and worry. He hated seeing his lover entertain men who cared less about her but only found pleasure in the joy she gave.

Bancroft was still stalking Rachel when his attention got abruptly diverted as a wave of black-suited figures flooded the club, their menacing presence casting an ominous shadow over the revelry. Panic erupted like wildfire. The previously raucous atmosphere transformed into a chaotic frenzy. Women were forcibly removed, and the deafening chaos drowned out their cries.

Rachel was among them, her eyes wide with fear. Instinct took over as Bancroft sprung into action, drawing his gun in one fluid motion. The weapon's weight felt familiar and comforting in his hand, a protection tool in the face of danger.

He manoeuvred through the crowd with the precision of a predator, his senses heightened, focused solely on one goal: rescuing Rachel.

Gunfire erupted, shattering the air with its explosive force. The acrid scent of gunpowder mingled with the tang of sweat and fear, forming an intoxicating cocktail that permeated the club. Bullets whizzed past Bancroft, their deadly intent a constant reminder of the stakes.

With every step and calculated movement, Bancroft wove through the chaos like a ghost. He sought temporary refuge behind overturned tables and broken chairs, utilizing the scant cover the club provided. The staccato rhythm of gunshots reverberated through his bones, creating an adrenaline-fueled symphony of danger and survival.

His finger caressed the trigger, each pulls releasing a burst of lethal intent. His aim was true, finding its mark on the black-suited assailants. He wounded one, causing him to stagger backwards, his howl of pain piercing through the pandemonium. But they were relentless, their onslaught unyielding.

They made it past the exit, Rachel lost in their fierce grip.

Bancroft's heart pounded in his chest, his breaths ragged and quick. Sweat trickled down his temple, mingling with the determination etched on his face. He knew time was slipping through his fingers like sand, each passing moment bringing Rachel closer to an uncertain fate.

Bancroft found himself stranded as the abductors retreated, disappearing into the murky shadows. His eyes darted across the room, scanning for his means of pursuit, for his escape from this crumbling stronghold of danger.

He watched them hop into the three-car fleet of Black Land Cruisers, shooting down the club's armed guards who dared to stand in their way.

Desperation threatened to consume Bancroft as he made it to the pavement, unsure what to do. When fate smiled at him, he was still glancing across for a possible means of mobility. A grey BMW screeched and halted right before him.

"Hop in," a female voice hollered above the chaos. It was Detective Elaine Murphy, her eyes ablaze with determination and urgency.

What the hell!

"Speak of the devil," Bancroft muttered, his voice a husky growl, a mixture of relief and surprise.

Without a second thought, he lunged into the car, the door slamming shut behind him, sealing his fate with a resounding thud. The tires squealed in protest as they peeled away from the club, leaving behind the chaos and uncertainty that had consumed Bancroft's world just moments before.

As they hurtled through the town's streets, the adrenaline coursing through Bancroft's veins began to subside, allowing him a moment to catch his breath. He stole a glance at Elaine, her expression a mask of determination, her hands firmly gripping the steering wheel.

"What the hell is happening, Elaine?" Bancroft demanded, his voice laced with frustration and urgency.

"We are all looking for an answer to the same question," Detective Elaine responded, her eyes firmly stuck to the road. She didn't want to ever miss the Land Cruisers ahead of them.

"Who could they be?"

Elaine's eyes flickered with a mix of trepidation and resolve. "I can't give you any answer right now, Bancroft— I mean, even if at all I knew them," she replied, her voice steady despite the turmoil. "But I promise you this: we'll get to the bottom. They're not getting away with her."

Bancroft nodded, a steely resolve settling deep within his bones. Despite the danger that loomed over them, he knew he couldn't afford to back down. Rachel's life hung in the balance, and his duty as her man demanded that he pull heaven and earth to have her out of the grip of those bloodthirsty men.

The car tore through the streets of Capeton, maintaining a not-too-far-nor-close proximity to the fleet ahead of them. She pressed down the accelerator, and the almost noiseless engine roared in symphony with the darkness that enveloped their path.

Bancroft clenched his fists, ready to face the unknown that awaited them. Rachel's abduction had thrust him further into a vortex of intrigue that threatened to consume them all. But he was undeterred, his determination unyielding.

Bancroft heard the cough of an engine behind them. While Detective Elaine peeped through the reflection of the rearview mirror, he spun around enough to get a glimpse of the full chassis of the incoming sound.

It was a car. One that looked familiar. He knew who it was as it came under the lights of one of the lone street lamps.

"Who the hell is that?"

"Hunter!"

But then, Hunter wasn't alone. He had company. A motorcycle, right behind him at full speed.

Bancroft didn't know who that was. But he sure knew that whoever it was, wasn't on their side.

"Shit!"

CHAPTER EIGHTEEN

THE CAR CHASE UNFOLDED like a blazing inferno, flames of adrenaline and danger licking at their heels. Bancroft never imagined that Detective Elaine Murphy possessed such untamed skill behind the wheel. She manoeuvred the car with the agility of a Formula One racer, navigating the treacherous streets with precision and fury.

As the engine roared, their tires screeched, leaving behind a trail of burning rubber. The abductors ahead were relentless, their vehicles forged ahead, increasing in speed but Detective Elaine was all out to close in on them like a ravenous predator.

Again, they remembered they were not alone in this race against time.

Detective Christopher Hunter, their backup, surged forward, his vehicle joining the chaotic pursuit. The cacophony of engines and sirens filled the air, blending into a symphony of raw power. The streets blurred as they tore through the Capeton, their determination propelling them forward.

It looked like a stretch race. The prize wasn't girls or money as in downtown Montebello. The prize was more rewarding and worth chasing.

Bancroft clenched his fists, his heart pounding with fear and exhilaration. The wind whipped against his face, carrying the scent of burning fuel and the thrill of the chase. They weaved through traffic, leaving startled drivers in their wake, their pursuit a blur of steel and determination.

But as if the abductors' desperation knew no bounds, another man on a motorbike joined the chase, his intentions clear as he aimed his gun at Bancroft's car.

Shit.

Bullets rained down upon them, shattering glass and puncturing metal. Bancroft retaliated in a burst of instinct, firing back at the motorcyclist. Their shots echoed through the streets as a deadly dance of survival unfolded.

Detective Hunter, assessing the situation with a hawk-like focus, lined up his shot. With unyielding precision, he fired a single round, the bullet finding its mark. The motorcyclist's body jerked backwards, his grip on the handlebars faltering. The bike veered off course, hurtling toward an isolated house. Metal crunched and splintered upon impact, the rider's fate sealed.

Too easy!

The chase continued, the abductors' vehicles splitting at a critical point. Two cars veered left while one broke away to the right. The urgency surged within Bancroft and Elaine as they knew Rachel was in one of the vehicles that had gone left.

"We can't let them escape, Elaine!" Bancroft shouted above the thunderous roar of the engines. "Rachel's life is on the line!"

Elaine's eyes flashed with unwavering determination. "We won't, Bancroft," she replied, her voice cutting through the chaos. "We'll chase them down. Keep an eye on the flanks."

Their cars swerved through the twisting labyrinth of the town streets, the sense of urgency propelling them forward. Detective Hunter, undeterred by the split in the pursuit, chose to follow the two cars that veered left, determined to assist in the rescue of Rachel. Bancroft could still see him speeding behind them.

The chase continued, a high-stakes game of cat and mouse played out with roaring engines and screeching tires. The town lights streaked past like fleeting glimpses of hope in the darkness. Bancroft and Elaine pushed their cars to the limits, weaving through traffic and defying the laws of speed and gravity.

Nothing else mattered at that point as long as no life was taken.

The two cars carrying Rachel fought tooth and nail to catch up with the fleet of Land cruisers ahead. They swerved and darted, navigating the Capeton's maze of streets recklessly. But Bancroft and Elaine were relentless, their resolve unshakable.

"We're gaining on them, Elaine!" Bancroft called out, and his voice tinged with exhilaration and desperation. "We can't let them slip away!"

Elaine's grip on the steering wheel tightened, her knuckles turning white. "Hold on tight, Bancroft," she replied, her voice filled with unwavering determination. "You might have tumbled a bit. We're almost there."

Tension hung heavy as the chase raced toward its climactic crescendo. The fate of Rachel, their target and ally, hung in the balance. The pursuit became a symphony of speed, adrenaline, and unwavering resolve.

Bancroft's focus narrowed, and his senses sharpened. He could almost taste victory, the sweet triumph of rescuing Rachel from the clutches of darkness. He felt Detective Elaine's fingers tighten around the steering wheel as his gaze locked on the taillights of the abductors' cars, determination etched into every line of his face.

The reading on the speedometer scared him a bit but that didn't matter.

Elaine's voice broke through the chaos, her words searing with urgency. "Bancroft, we need to coordinate our moves. We have to corner them, cut off their escape routes."

Bancroft nodded, a fire ignited in his eyes. "I'm with you."

"She's in the first car. Get the one behind. I need the tire inflated. Don't stop shooting!" Elaine ordered as Bancroft tucked his face out the window, his gun trained forward.

Their cars closed the distance, closing in on the two vehicles that held Rachel captive. They manoeuvred through the flanks of the road, anticipating the abductors' next moves, exploiting every gap and opportunity that presented itself. The pursuit intensified, the air crackling with anticipation.

Suddenly, the lead car veered sharply to the left, taking a narrow side street. The second car followed suit. Bancroft and Elaine did the same, their tires screeching against the pavement as they pursued relentlessly. The abductors' desperation was palpable, their manoeuvres becoming more reckless and desperate.

That was the car that had Rachel. Bancroft saw Detective Hunter making the same move, still heading in their direction.

"We're almost there, Bancroft!" Elaine's voice rang out, determination lacing her words. "Just the tires. We need her alive!"

Did she have to tell me that? Does she even know we're in an affair?

Bancroft gritted his teeth, his heart pounding with anticipation and fear. He had come too far to let Rachel slip away. The pursuit reached a fever pitch, a flurry of twisting and turning as if fate herself danced on the knife's edge.

But just when it seemed like victory was within reach, tragedy struck. A gunshot echoed through the air, shattering the tension-filled atmosphere. One of the abductors' cars veered out of control, crashing into a fiery spectacle that consumed it entirely.

After the second car exploded, the car chase smelled no deviation in speed or intent. It only grew tougher. Bancroft could feel his heart pounding in his chest, matching the rhythm of the roaring engine beneath him. Again, he stole glances at Detective Elaine, imagining how she got so skilled behind the wheel.

Bancroft clenched his fists, his knuckles turning white, as he fought against the G-forces pushing him back into his seat. The wind whipped against his face, hard and winding.

But as if the abductors' desperation knew no bounds, the trunk of the last car suddenly swung open, revealing a deadly surprise. It was a trick Detective Elaine and Bancroft didn't see coming.

Steel caltrops spilt onto the road, creating a treacherous obstacle. Elaine's eyes widened as she saw the danger, and her grip on the steering wheel tightened. With lightning-fast reflexes, she swerved, trying to evade the caltrops, but it was too late.

The car hit the caltrops, its tires punctured, and its momentum sent it careening off the road. The world spun in a dizzying haze of chaos and violence as the car flipped, tumbling end over end before crashing into the open field nearby. Metal screamed in protest, mingling with the shattering of glass and the impact of their bodies colliding with the unforgiving interior of the vehicle.

Bancroft's head swam, his vision blurred, but he knew there was no time for weakness. With a surge of adrenaline, he forced open his door, crawling out of the wreckage, his senses heightened by the urgency of the situation. But he wasn't strong enough. He crashed back to the ground in absolute exhaustion.

Detective Christopher Hunter, his instincts on high alert, had witnessed the crash unfold. He halted his pursuit, screeching his vehicle to a stop. Without hesitation, he rushed toward the overturned car, his movements quick and purposeful.

Hunter could hear Bancroft and Elaine struggling to free themselves as he approached the wreckage. With a burst of strength, he pried open the jammed door, his eyes scanning the interior in search of Rachel. But to his dismay, she was nowhere to be found.

Hunter's eyes met Bancroft's as he lay weak and slightly conscious of what was happening around him. The weight of the situation settled heavily upon them.

Though shaken by the crash, Detective Elaine pushed aside her pain and joined their resolve. She erupted out of a stash of grass and staggered upward, her head soaked with blood.

"Where's Rachel?" Bancroft asked in a subtle tone.

"They took her," Detective Hunter responded.

Did they take her?

CHAPTER NINETEEN

BANCROFT LOGAN COULDN'T tear his eyes away from Rachel, the enchanting stripper who commanded the stage at the club at Central Capeton. The allure of her movements, the way her body swayed with an intoxicating rhythm, ignited a fire within him that refused to be quenched at least not by anybody else.

The soft, dim lighting caressed her flawless form, highlighting every curve, every dip, and Bancroft found himself drawn to her like a moth to a flame.

Their eyes locked across the room, a magnetic connection sparking between them. Rachel's lips curled into a sly smile, a silent invitation that Bancroft couldn't resist. With a determined stride, he made his way through the crowd, his heart pounding as he closed the distance between them.

The charged atmosphere crackled with anticipation as their bodies stood mere inches apart. The music's bass throbbed through their veins, mirroring the rush of desire that consumed them both. With a voice heavy with longing, Bancroft leaned in closer, his words a whisper against the cacophony of the club.

"Rachel," he murmured, his voice laced with curiosity and desire. "Something about you has captured my attention, something I can't explain."

Her eyes, filled with mischief and vulnerability, locked with his. The corner of her mouth lifted in a seductive smile, and her voice, a silky purr, brushed against his ear. "And what might that be, Hero Bancroft?"

Hero Bancroft?

He hesitated momentarily, his gaze tracing the enticing curve of her lips, before finding the words to respond. "It's the way you move," he confessed, his voice a low rasp. "Your every step, every sway, ignites a fire within me. It's a fire I can no longer ignore."

A flicker of excitement danced in her eyes, and Rachel took his hand in hers without a word. Together, they slipped away from the crowd, seeking solace and privacy in the dimly lit restroom. The air hummed with anticipation as the door closed behind them, shutting out the noise and distractions of the club.

They didn't need it!

In the confined space, their bodies gravitated toward each other, aching to fulfil the desires that had ignited between them. Time seemed to slow as their lips met in a searing kiss, an exploration of heat and longing.

Hot.

Adrenaline-inducing.

Breathtaking.

It was a collision of passion, a melding of souls as their tongues danced with wild fervour, trading fluids without freckles of guilt.

The two didn't have to go haywire back at the club's restroom. They took it to Bancroft Apartment. There, hell was let loose.

It began from the doorpost, swivelled towards the couch and ended at his king-size bed.

The perfect destination.

Bancroft's hands roamed Rachel's body, tracing the soft curves that haunted his thoughts. His fingertips trailed along her waist, leaving a fire trail in their wake. The silkiness of her skin beneath his touch was an intoxicating revelation, fueling the flames of desire that burned deep within him.

Rachel's fingers tangled in his hair, pulling him closer as their bodies moulded together. The scent of her perfume, a heady blend of jasmine and musk, filled his senses, heightening the intensity of their connection. Her lips tasted of temptation and urgency, a decadent feast he couldn't resist.

He wanted to eat her up. To devour her.

Desire surged between them, a hunger that couldn't be sated. Bancroft lifted Rachel onto the countertop, their eyes locked in a shared understanding of their unspoken desires. The cool surface pressed against her back, starkly contrasting the scorching heat that radiated between them.

Their clothing became an unnecessary barrier to the pleasures they sought. With an eagerness that bordered on desperation, they shed their garments, revealing their bare vulnerability to each other. Every inch of exposed skin was an invitation, a canvas for exploration and indulgence.

Bancroft's hands worshipped Rachel's form, his touch igniting electric currents of pleasure with every caress. His fingers trailed along the curves of her breasts, teasing, tantalizing, before descending further, tracing patterns of longing along her thighs. Her soft gasps and gentle moans fueled his desire, his body aching to taste the ecstasy she offered.

Lust and adoration intertwined as their bodies moved in perfect synchrony. Each touch and kiss spoke volumes of their shared longing and the depths of their passion. The room became a sanctuary of sensation, their intertwined forms a masterpiece of desire.

As their bodies danced to the rhythm of their shared passion, time ceased to exist. Moans and whispers filled the air, harmonizing with the symphony of their desires. The restroom walls reverberated with their symphony of pleasure, their connection transcending the physical.

Bancroft' hands had been exploring. It finally made it to the epicentre. The apple of her garden. His lips followed afterwards, sapping the caramel-like juices like pineapple nectar.

Isn't it?

As he got down there with his third leg, he felt the depth of her like he never got a chance to. She felt his shaft too. All of it. It felt like a frenzy more powerful than the drowsiness from the remnants of Vodka.

It became a rhythm. Every thrust and withdrawal left a message. A subtle one.

In that intimate space, Bancroft and Rachel found solace and fulfilment. Their bodies melded together, and every sensation heightened, every touch electric.

He came.

She came.

Tragic explosion.

The world outside faded away as they immersed themselves in the depths of their desires, losing themselves in the intoxicating dance of their love. It was like the dreadful hands of Whiskey numbing their bodies and making every other thing cease to exist.

As their breaths mingled and their bodies intertwined, they knew this connection was more than a passing flame. It was a spark that had ignited their souls, forever intertwining their paths. And in that moment, as their bodies reached the pinnacle of ecstasy, they surrendered to the boundless depths of their love, knowing that their desires would continue to intertwine long after this passionate encounter.

When Bancroft remembered how Rachel walked through the door. He knew that that could be his best memory of their time together.

Nothing ever felt better than those moments.

CHAPTER TWENTY

EXHAUSTED AND DRAINED, Bancroft knew he needed time to recuperate, both physically and mentally. As a PTSD patient, rest was a necessary ritual if he wanted to regain his strength. But his mind couldn't help but dwell on Rachel and the potential dangers she might face.

Where the hell did they take her to?

Detectives Christopher Hunter and Elaine Murphy stood guard in the hallway leading to Bancroft' bed, their watchful eyes scanning for any signs of danger. Over time, Detective Hunter had come to accept Elaine, recognizing her pivotal role in their efforts to locate Rachel.

Together, they remained vigilant, ready to defend their comrade. Although Detective Elaine suffered an injury herself, hers wasn't too bad according to the doctor. Bancroft needed more time since he had a slight head injury to the walls of his cranium.

But even with their watchful presence, an attacker managed to infiltrate the same room they secured like the Pentagon.

Disguised as a nurse, the figure moved with calculated precision, blending seamlessly into the hospital environment. Bancroft, pretending to be asleep, observed her every move, his instincts on high alert. Something about her demeanour set off alarms in his mind.

They are everywhere!

Bancroft's heart raced as the nurse approached, her eyes darting around the room. He could sense danger lurking beneath her seemingly innocent facade. She switched syringes with the expertise of a seasoned professional, her target set on his arm. But Bancroft was ready, his frustration fueling a surge of adrenaline within him.

Just moments before, he had witnessed Detective Christopher discreetly place a gun under his pillow, a silent act of precaution. But now, as Bancroft reached for the weapon, his hand grasped at thin air. The gun was gone, vanished without a trace. Panic gripped him momentarily as he realized his vulnerability.

"Who took the gun?"

Bancroft would have to rely on his physical prowess alone in a split-second decision. He launched himself at the nurse with lightning-fast reflexes, engaging her in a desperate fight for survival. Blows were exchanged, the sound of impact echoing through the hospital room. The nurse, clearly skilled in hand-to-hand combat, matched Bancroft blow for blow, her moves fluid and precise.

Bancroft' biggest fear was sapped. The syringe. His first kick sent it crashing to the floor.

He gritted his teeth, his muscles straining with each strike. He ducked and weaved, dodging her punches and countering with well-aimed blows of his own. His training kicked in, instincts guiding his movements as he fought to protect himself, uncover the truth, and stay alive to fight his fights.

The room became a battleground, their struggle a dance of aggression and resilience. They circled each other, their eyes locked in a deadly gaze. Bancroft could see the nurse's determination and unwavering resolve to fulfil her sinister mission.

Who hired her to kill me?

"You won't succeed," Bancroft growled, his voice laced with defiance. "I won't let you harm me or anyone I care about."

The nurse smirked, a cold glint in her eyes. "You underestimate me, Bancroft," she taunted, her voice dripping with malevolence. "I've faced far greater adversaries than you. You're just a pawn in a much larger game."

A pawn?

In a much larger game?

Bancroft lunged forward, his fist connecting with the nurse's jaw. The impact reverberated through the room, momentarily stunning her. It was a small victory, a glimmer of hope amidst the chaos. He slammed the steel drug tray right against her flat nose.

"I may be a pawn, but I'm a pawn who fights back," Bancroft retorted, his voice fierce. "And I won't let you win."

The nurse's lips curled into a cruel smile as she countered, striking Bancroft with a swift kick to the abdomen. The blow knocked the wind out of him, momentarily weakening his defences. But he refused to relent, summoning his strength and fighting through the pain.

He hadn't healed. He could feel the pain within his core.

Their battle intensified, each strike fueled by desperation and determination. Bancroft fought with a ferocity born out of love and loyalty, refusing to let Rachel become another victim of darkness. The nurse matched him blow for blow, her expertise and skill testing his limits.

Elaine and Christopher, stationed just outside the room, exchanged worried glances. The struggle echoed through the corridor, a symphony of violence and survival.

Something's wrong, Detective Hunter thought. He felt it.

As they burst into the room, Detectives Elaine and Hunter's presence provided Bancroft with much-needed support. The nurse's attention momentarily diverted, and Bancroft seized the opportunity to launch a powerful strike, sending her reeling backwards. It was the hardest hit he gave her. He complimented it by putting a ten-millimetre right into the back of her neck.

But before they could celebrate their advantage, the nurse swiftly recovered, her eyes burning with rage. She lunged at Bancroft with renewed ferocity, her movements fueled by desperation from her faltering plan.

Is she human?

Elaine's gaze locked onto the nurse, her finger tightening on the trigger of her gun. "Enough is enough," she said, her voice filled with conviction.

In a heartbeat, a gunshot reverberated through the room. The bullet found its mark, tearing through the nurse's leg and causing her to crumble in pain.

But to the shock of everyone present, Elaine didn't stop there.

Driven by adrenaline and determination, Elaine stepped forward, her eyes fixed on the nurse. She raised her gun, her finger steady on the trigger. Time seemed to slow at that moment as the room held its breath.

A single shot rang out, cutting through the air with lethal precision. The nurse's body jerked backwards, her eyes wide with shock, as the bullet tore through her skull. Silence descended upon the room, broken only by the echoes of the gunshot that sealed the nurse's fate.

Still catching his breath, Bancroft looked at Elaine with gratitude and disbelief. "You... you saved my life," he stammered, his voice filled with awe and relief.

That's not what I intended to say!

Elaine met his gaze, her eyes reflecting the weight of their circumstances. "We're a team, Bancroft," she replied, her voice tinged with sadness and determination. "We have to protect each other. We can't afford to take any chances."

Detective Christopher, his gaze fixed on the nurse's lifeless body, felt a surge of conflicting emotions. Anger swirled within him as he considered the lost opportunity for vital information. Yet, deep down, he knew that Elaine had acted in the heat of the moment, driven by the need to save their comrade.

"I understand why you did it," Detective Hunter finally spoke, his voice laced with frustration and acceptance. "We were up against the wall, and you made a split-second decision. We can't change what happened now."

Elaine nodded her expression a mix of determination and regret. "I had to make a choice," she replied, her voice tinged with a hint of sadness. "I couldn't risk losing you, Bancroft. But I know the consequences of my actions. I mean. I could blame it on adrenaline but I don't justify my evils."

Bancroft, still catching his breath, nodded in agreement. "We can't let this setback deter us," he replied, determination burning in his eyes.

"Rachel's life is on the line, and we owe it to her to push forward, no matter the cost."

But as they stood in the aftermath of their fight, a sombre realization settled upon them. The nurse's death left them with no immediate leads or direct path. They were back to square one, faced with the daunting task of finding Rachel without a clear starting point.

Detective Hunter knew how angry that would make the Chief feel! His gaze hardened as he glanced at the lifeless body of the nurse. "We lost our chance at answers," he said, his voice tinged with frustration. "What's the way forward?"

Elaine's eyes met Hunter's, a steely resolve burning within her. "We found her," she said, her voice unwavering. "We can't afford to dwell on what we've lost. We'll regroup, reassess, and find a new angle to pursue. There's something out there!"

Though physically exhausted, Bancroft felt a renewed determination surge through his veins. Rachel's face flashed in his mind, fueling his resolve.

A sense of purpose filled the room as they prepared to continue their mission. The fight against the unknown had only begun, but they were stronger together.

Stronger together!

We've always been!

How did these two ever cross each other's lane?

CHAPTER TWENTY-ONE

DEEP IN THE HEART OF AN AUSTRIAN rainforest, Lieutenant Juniors Bancroft Logan and Christopher Hunter found themselves embroiled in a high-stakes mission. The peacefulness of their training exercises was abruptly shattered when reports surfaced of rebel forces seeking refuge in the dense wilderness.

The rebels launched a missile into an Army base, recording many casualties. The radar tracked them to the point where they found succour right inside the rain and knew they wouldn't be tracked easily due to poor signal.

"Tear down the damn woods. I need him alive," the commander had commanded.

It was a tumultuous day, the sky heavy with dark clouds, as the team prepared for an unprecedented operation. As the rain poured down upon them, soaking their combat uniforms and muddying the forest floor, Bancroft and Hunter stood side by side, their gazes focused and unwavering.

They barely knew each other except at drill grounds and shooting ranges back at the base.

Their mission was clear: neutralize the rebel forces and extract the main suspect, the leader responsible for inciting violence and the attack on the base. The rainforest became a battleground, it's towering trees and lush undergrowth transforming into cover and obstacle.

Soldiers were trained that way. To make a weapon out of anything.

With his strong build and unwavering determination, Lieutenant Junior Hunter took the lead, his tactical prowess honed from years of military training. Lieutenant Juniors Bancroft, his eyes sharp and alert, followed closely, a steadfast partner at his side. The two barely knew each other but the growing camaraderie they were beginning to build seemed like one that'd be built on trust— the best friendship by comrades that expanded even beyond military service are those forged through countless missions where their lives depended on each other.

That was the direction Bancroft and Hunter were leading.

The rain battered against their faces as they ventured deeper into the forest, navigating through treacherous terrain and evading enemy patrols. Each step brought them closer to their objective, their focus unyielding despite the danger lurking around every corner.

Suddenly, a shot rang out, cutting through the air like a sharp crack of thunder. John Bobson, a highly skilled sniper positioned in a strategic vantage point, had just made his first headshot.

The rebel forces were momentarily thrown into disarray, allowing Bancroft and Hunter to seize the opportunity to infiltrate their ranks. It was a well-mapped distraction that'd guarantee a flawless extraction.

With their hearts pounding, the Bancroft and Hunter moved swiftly, executing coordinated manoeuvres that showcased their tactical expertise. They engaged in close-quarter combat, their movements fluid and instinctual.

Each enemy they encountered was neutralized swiftly as they seamlessly covered each other's backs, their trust in one another unwavering.

Their target was the leader of the rebels!

Their mission took them deeper into the heart of the rainforest, where the rebels had entrenched themselves. The air was tense as gunfire erupted around them, the sound merging with the steady beat of rain against leaves. Amidst the chaos, Bancroft and Hunter communicated with military precision, their commands sharp and concise.

"Bancroft, move left and provide covering fire!"

"Hunter, flank them from the right! We need to push them back!"

Their voices cut through the cacophony, carrying the weight of authority. They moved as one, their actions synchronized and purposeful. Their bond was forged in the crucible of battle, an unspoken understanding transcending words.

They fought with a seamless synergy, their movements complementing each other flawlessly.

Bancroft would provide suppressive fire, pinning down the rebels with precise shots while Hunter manoeuvred through the dense foliage, taking out adversaries with lethal accuracy. Their tactics were honed and precise from years of rigorous training and shared experiences.

Born killers!

Their targets fell one by one, and the sounds of battle drowned out their cries. The rebels, overwhelmed by the sheer force and efficiency of Bancroft and Hunter's assault, began to retreat. Sensing the tide turning in their favour, the two soldiers pushed forward, relentlessly pursuing the rebel leader.

Through the rain-soaked forest, they pressed on, their senses heightened, their instincts sharp. As they closed in on their target, a clearing emerged from the dense foliage, revealing the rebel leader surrounded by his loyal followers.

Hunter's eyes narrowed, his grip tightening on his weapon. He signalled Bancroft to hold position while positioning himself for a clear shot. With the surgeon's precision, Hunter aimed, his finger caressing the trigger, and with a controlled exhale, he squeezed it. The shot echoed through the rainforest as the rebel leader fell, a silent testament to Hunter's lethal skill.

First, what rang in his head was the commander's first sentence.

"Bring him alive…"

The second one followed a few seconds after.

"Or dead!"

With their objective neutralized, Bancroft and Hunter moved swiftly to extract themselves and the three other members of their five-man extraction team from the heart of the rainforest. The rain continued to pour, obscuring their vision and turning the forest floor into a treacherous quagmire. They pushed forward, relying on their instincts and the unwavering trust they shared.

John Bobson, the sniper who had provided crucial support throughout the mission, joined them as they regrouped. He was the sixth member of the team.

Finally, they reached the rendezvous point where the rest of their team awaited. The familiar faces of their comrades greeted them, relief etched on their weary features. The mission had succeeded, thanks in no small part to Bancroft and Hunter's valour and unwavering resolve.

As they gathered around, fatigue and adrenaline still breezing through their veins, the team exchanged stories and accolades. The respect in their eyes as they looked at Bancroft and Hunter was palpable, a testament to the incredible display of skill and bravery they had witnessed.

They were small gods!

Bancroft and Hunter exchanged glances, their eyes reflecting a deep understanding beyond the battlefield. They had fought side by side, putting their lives on the line for a common cause, and in doing so, a bond had formed. It was a brotherhood forged in the crucible of battle, a bond that transcended the confines of a mission.

"Always wanted to be a soldier?" Hunter asked Bancroft as they sank to the group, munching pieces of dried crunchy desserts."

Bancroft nodded in affirmative. "Every day of my life!"

"You were born for it?" Hunter chuckled.

"I grew up in the barracks. In the face of battles and wars, with a single mother. She was a Cavalry Scout herself. E8. Got married to a Marine. He didn't make it home after a campaign somewhere in Iraq!"

"I'm sorry about that," Hunter chipped in.

Bancroft chuckled." Come on. It's fine. That was a long time ago. Before I was even born," he paused and flung another Chun of dessert into his mouth. "He had no idea she was pregnant. So, he never got to see it! But as I grew up, I felt strength when she said I would be as fearless as him. "
"You are, Bancroft!"

Bancroft nodded. "Yeah. Like you, did you know what it felt to have a father?"

Hunter reached for him for his dog tags. They were three instead of two. He pulled it out. "Here," he drew Bancroft's Attention to it. "He believed that only cowards don't serve in the military. He fought in Kuwait. He said I can always be the best soldier if I believe I could be!"

Bancroft nodded, his lips pulling into a low smile. "Your mom?"

"She passed in my 12th grade. Yeah. So, I think I had a fair share of a mother-son bond. I always loved her. We all love the owners of the pair of breasts we first suckled.

"Bancroft," Hunter said, his voice filled with admiration. "I couldn't have asked for a better partner. You've got the heart of a lion."

Bancroft, a modest smile gracing his lips, nodded in acknowledgement. "And you, Hunter, are a force to all lean.

Their words were simple yet carried immense weight. At that moment, a friendship was solidified amidst the camaraderie and shared sense of purpose.

Now Private Bancroft and Homicide Detective Hunter, they two maintained the bond even after military service.

They had become more than partners.

They were brothers, bound by their shared experiences and profound respect for each other.

In battle and solitude.

As they sat together, their exhausted bodies finding solace in the company of their comrades, they knew that this mission was just the beginning.

The rainforest had tested them, and they had emerged victorious. With their bond forged in the heat of battle, they were ready to face whatever challenges lay ahead, side by side.

That bond was what Bancroft preferred to protect more than anything else.

CHAPTER TWENTY-TWO

BANCROFT SAT AT A SMALL TABLE tucked away in the corner of the cosy café, his fingers clasped around his coffee mug. The rich aroma of freshly brewed coffee mingled with the tantalizing scents of baked goods, creating an inviting atmosphere within the bustling café. The soft lighting cast a warm glow, offering solace amidst the cacophony of the city.

Across from Bancroft, Mr Holmes, his contractor at Midas Securities, watched him intently, a mug of coffee untouched in front of him. Holmes was a man who thrived on opportunities, always seeking the next venture. Yet, his latest proposition tugged at Bancroft' conscience, sparking a battle within his heart.

"Bancroft," Holmes began, his voice laced with urgency and persuasion, "I understand your dedication to the murder investigation, but sometimes, it's necessary to shift focus. I have a new case—an intriguing homicide in a town about four miles from Montebello. It requires your expertise, and I believe it could be a breakthrough for you."

Or for us!

Bancroft raised his mug to his lips, taking a slow sip of his coffee, using the momentary silence to gather his thoughts. He observed the patrons bustling about the café, each engaged in their conversations, oblivious to the weighty decision that Bancroft grappled with. The clinking of cups, the gentle hum of chatter, and the soft background music created a soothing aura that provided a brief respite from their intense conversation.

Finally, Bancroft placed his mug back on the saucer, meeting Holmes' gaze with determination and hesitation. "Mr Holmes, I appreciate the offer but can't simply let go of the murder investigation. The victim's family deserves justice, and I owe it to them to see it through. It's not a case I can abandon lightly. It all started with me."

Holmes leaned forward, his eyes searching Bancroft' face for any sign of acquiescence. "I understand your dedication, Bancroft, but our hands are tied sometimes. There are forces at play beyond our control. This new case is time-sensitive, and it requires your immediate attention. I need you to set aside the murder investigation for now."

There it came. The request usually sounded like a command. It was one of the many things Bancroft dreaded about his job with Midas Securities.

As the weight of Holmes' request command hung heavy, a commotion erupted from a nearby table. Two men engaged in a heated argument, their voices escalating into shouts. The once serene café transformed into a chaotic battleground of words.

Bancroft and Holmes momentarily pause their conversation, their eyes drawn to the unfolding scene. Waiters and waitresses hurried over, their attempts to diffuse the situation heightening the tension in the room. The clash of voices, the clattering of plates, and the frantic footsteps mingled with the aroma of spilt coffee and the sturdy energy of conflict.

The interruption gave Bancroft and Holmes a brief respite, a chance to observe their surroundings and reflect on their choices. Bancroft gazed at the chaotic scene, his mind momentarily pulled away from the weight of the murder investigation and the crossroads he found himself standing at. The sounds, smells, and sights of the café became a metaphor for the choices he faced—fragments of a larger narrative waiting to be understood.

Once the altercation subsided and a fragile calm settled over the café again, Bancroft refocused on Holmes. "Mr Holmes, I can't ignore my gut on this one. This murder investigation has consumed me; there's more to it than meets the eye. I believe connections and truths are waiting to be unearthed. I can't turn my back on that."

Holmes sighed, the frustration etched on his face slowly giving way to resignation. He tapped his fingers on the table, his eyes drifting across the café as if searching for solace in the surrounding environment. The lingering aroma of coffee and the comforting buzz of conversation offered a brief respite from their intense negotiation.

"Ever thought of how turning this down will affect our contract?" Mr Homes aired. It was the part of the conversation Bancroft had waited to hear.

"It'd impact solely on the clause and understand that. I'll stick to the relief rule. My attorney will reach out accordingly."

Mr Holmes was slightly taken aback. Ever since he introduced him to the corridors of private investigators, he had always seen resistance from Bancroft. But none came close to accepting a downward pay cut just to stick to a case that won't earn him a dime!

"You sure you wanna do this for you!"

Bancroft took another sip off his mug. A long one this time. "I think I know what I want when it comes."

Another silence hovered around them as the two sat in silence. They stared at nothing in particular but had thoughts rushing through his head. To Bancroft, backing out of the new case was a monetary loss but getting to the root of the folding murder superseded every other thing. Meanwhile, Mr Holmes must have had one major feeling; the fear of losing money and more honest clientele.

"You've always been a tenacious investigator, Bancroft," Holmes acknowledged, his voice tinged with admiration and disappointment. "I respect your dedication, even if I don't entirely agree with it. Just remember, the path you've chosen may have consequences."

Bancroft' relationship with Mr. Holmes is traced back to four years ago. He had helped an older lady whack a pickpocket in a mall, shredding his lips and knocking the wind out of his lungs as he bullied the gutful jerk who stole from someone old enough to be called his grandmother.

Mr Holmes later met Bancroft at the counter, where he had his grocery sized and priced. He shared his card and walked through the door, leaving an impression that got Bancroft wanting to know more about him. Two months down the line, Mr Holmes linked him with Midas Securities, where he again began a new phase of his life in a field not too close not far from the military where he originally belonged.

Bancroft leaned forward, his eyes meeting Holmes with unwavering resolve. "I'm aware of the risks, Mr. Holmes. But I've always embraced the shadows in search of truth. I won't shy away from the consequences, whatever they may be."

The café's atmosphere seemed to shift as if acknowledging the weight of their conversation. The comforting aroma of freshly ground coffee beans mingled with the soft murmurs of conversations, enveloping them in a cocoon of familiarity and possibility.

As Bancroft and Holmes concluded their meeting, their conversation lingered in the air, the unspoken understanding between them leaving room for further collaboration, albeit on different paths. They rose from their seats, the echo of their decisions resonating within the walls of the café.

Bancroft stepped out into the bustling Central Capeton, his mind focused on the murder investigation he refused to abandon. The taste of coffee still clung to his lips, fueling his determination to seek justice amidst the shadows that awaited him. The chaos and interruptions of the café mirrored the challenges he would face, but he was ready to confront them head-on, trusting his instincts to guide him through the tangled web of the case.

Nothing else mattered.

As Bancroft watched Mr Holme leave the cafe, the soft breeze slapped a memory through his head.

It wasn't just the pickpocket incident at the mall that got him a permanent contract with Midas Securities without being on probation.

It was his first job outside Capeton and Montebello that did.

A kidnap at Matilton.

A beautiful small town about four miles away, Montebello.

CHAPTER TWENTY-THREE

ARMS CROSSED, BANCROFT LOGAN and Sheriff Jakes Mandta of Matilton Sheriff Department sat across a dimly lit table from Mayor Frank Bucket, the former leader of the town now embroiled in a personal tragedy. The room exuded an air of tension as the three men locked eyes, each aware of the weight of the situation.

Since joining Midas Securities, that was Bancroft' first case outside Capeton and Montebello. He had been to Matilton once or twice. It is a town twice about half the size of Capeton and a quarter of Montebello but known for its beautiful views of Lake Boggle, hike trails, amusement parks and quite popular politicians. It was a town that once produced a Congress Speaker.

Speaking of popular politicians, Frank Bucket was one of them. The Australian-American became the mayor of Matilton some years back. His election was popularly known as that which was born of popular demand. He was a Harvard law graduate who dedicated his Legal Aid Foundation to seeking justice for innocent people on death row. The tale of the statewide abolishment of capital punishment couldn't be whole without his input.

But, the same Frank Bucket got whipped so hard when his pregnant wife was abducted by unknown men at the mall entrance, less than a mile from his residence.

Bancroft leaned forward, his piercing gaze fixed on the mayor. "Mayor Bucket, we need your full cooperation to find your wife. We understand that she has been abducted and need any information you can provide."

Mayor Bucket's face betrayed a mix of anguish and frustration as he clasped his hands together. "I assure you, Mr. Logan, I had no hand in my wife's disappearance. She means everything to me. I love her."

Sheriff Mandta studied the mayor intently, his voice firm yet empathetic. "Mayor Bucket, we believe you. But we need to know everything. Did the abductors contact you?"

He nodded. "They contacted me. The next morning after her disappearance."

"What do they want?"

Mayor Bucket's gaze drifted momentarily before he met their eyes once more. "Yes, they called me. They were cold and calculating but they demanded a ransom of $700,000 for Sarah's safe return."

The amount was shockingly hefty. At first, it seemed strange for kidnappers in a small town to name such an amount for a ransom but at the same time, it boiled down to who's involved. They knew the former Mayor could afford whatever price they named.

"Any other specifics? Like warnings? How to make the payment?"

"They warned me not to involve the police, to keep it discreet."

They never want the Police!
Bancroft furrowed his brow, his mind already racing with possibilities. "Did they provide any instructions on how to deliver the ransom?"

The mayor nodded, his voice heavy with concern. "They instructed me to await further instructions at a specific drop-off point tomorrow night. They warned that any attempt to involve law enforcement or deviate from their instructions would result in dire consequences."

Sheriff Mandta leaned back in his chair, contemplating the gravity of the situation. "Mayor Bucket, we understand your predicament, but we need to work together to ensure your wife's safe return. We will set up a surveillance operation with our team close by to ensure her safety. Trust us to handle this. We want their next call recorded— every word of the call scrutinized. We'd engage our telecommunications unit to test-track the signals. We'll certainly get those rogues and bring Sarah home safely. "

Mayor Bucket's shoulders slumped with a mix of relief and uncertainty. "I don't know what I would do without Sarah. Please, do whatever it takes to bring her back to me."

Bancroft nodded solemnly. "We will, Mayor. But we need your utmost cooperation. It could be crucial to the investigation if you can provide any other information that might help us, no matter how seemingly insignificant."

Mayor Bucket hesitated momentarily before a flicker of realization crossed his face. "There was one thing... During the call, I heard a dog barking in the background. It sounded distant as if the call was being made somewhere else."

Bancroft and Sheriff Mandta exchanged glances, recognizing the significance of the mayor's revelation. Bancroft leaned forward, his voice filled with determination. "Thank you, Mayor. That information might prove vital. We will do everything we can to bring Sarah back safely."

The surveillance operation was up and running. They staked out the designated drop-off point, ensuring every detail was meticulously planned for Sarah's safety. The tension mounted, the seconds ticking away as they waited for the pivotal moment.

As the sun set on the designated day, a call came in, confirming the abductors' demand for the ransom drop-off. Bancroft and Sheriff Mandta's teams positioned themselves nearby, hidden in the shadows, ready to spring into action immediately.

The night air grew heavy with anticipation as Bancroft and Sheriff Mandta observed the scene from a discreet vantage point. A black SUV approached, its headlights illuminating the deserted location. Two men emerged, their faces concealed beneath masks, their sinister intentions predictable even in the darkness.

Bancroft wasn't sure, but he felt a slight disparity between the shape of the men who just alighted from the SUV and those from the CCTV footage at the mall where Sarah was abducted.

Bancroft clenched his fists, his eyes fixed on the unfolding scene. He signalled to the waiting teams, their presence a silent reassurance in the face of danger. The moment had arrived.

Bancroft' eyes were out for everything worth searching for but most importantly, Sarah. He couldn't sign off her. It was there he began to sense foul play.

It could be a set-up.

As the exchange took place, tensions escalated. A sudden sense of foreboding filled the air as the abductors hesitated, suspicion etched in their eyes. In a split second, chaos erupted. Gunfire erupted from both sides, illuminating the night with blinding flashes and thunderous echoes.

Bancroft, Sheriff Mandta, and their teams unleashed a barrage of bullets, their aim true and resolute. They fought with precision, each movement calculated and measured, determined to overcome the abductors and rescue Sarah.

Amidst the hail of gunfire, Bancroft charged forward, adrenaline pumping through his veins. He breached the hideout, confronting the abductors face-to-face, their eyes filled with rage and desperation. Shots rang out, echoes reverberating through the corridors as the firefight intensified.

Through the chaos and smoke, Bancroft caught a glimpse of a woman in the backseat of the car. She was terrified, her eyes wide with fear but filled with hope.

Bancroft called off the shooting from his end. The men were the only ones firing. They made it ahead. They were never to be followed.

Sheriff Mandta saw from a distance. Bancroft saw it too. Another vehicle from the adjoining lane stopped by and picked them up.

Bancroft saw no need to fight them. They were pawns. They were a decoy. When he noticed the lady behind wasn't Sarah, he knew it was a lame move to chase them.

Bancroft had stuck a bag with perfectly carved papers with $5,000 bills used to coat the top of the bag. He felt it was a smart move. But the kidnappers hired two men in an SUV. Kidnapped another woman and stuffed her stomach with bed sheets to see if the Mayor would keep his promise of not involving the cops in the operation.

It failed.

What would they do to her now?

Nothing positive came from the series of test runs on the SUV. The men were heavily gloved that they left nothing behind. Not a drop of blood. The woman, the fake Sarah, was reunited with her family, while the car's license plate number was fake. It led nowhere and nobody.

But hope sprung out of the blues. It was a call within Matilton. A man phoned to report something suspicious.

It was the beginning of the end.

The moon hung high in the ink-black sky, casting a pale glow over the quiet streets of the Matilton. Bancroft and Sheriff Jakes Mandta stood in the dimly lit garage, their eyes scanning the surroundings for any sign of the trapped Sarah. The tension was breathtaking as they prepared to confront the two men who had callously held her captive.

Yes. He knew they were two. Just two greedy men were dreaming of getting an illegal share of the Mayor's wealth. The phone calls further confirmed the suspicion of the random caller. Although weak, the signal was around Howard Street.

Later, they were joined by a dog trainer named Ethan Mitchell. He wanted the one who phoned the Sheriff's Department. He had stumbled upon a disturbing scene while walking with his loyal companion, Max. Ethan had noticed something off about the men, their furtive glances and nervous demeanour raising alarm bells in his mind. Recognizing the need for swift action, he had reached out to nine-one-one.

As Bancroft's team approached the nondescript house, its exterior blending seamlessly with the surrounding neighbourhood, Bancroft felt a surge of adrenaline coursing through his veins. The sound of a barking dog echoed in the distance, a reminder of the loyal companion who had led them to this pivotal moment.

It also echoed the observation from Mayor Frank Bucket during his interview. Bancroft could recall hai exact words.

I heard a dog barking in the background. It sounded distant as if the call was being made elsewhere.

The front door creaked open, revealing a dimly lit living room adorned with tattered furniture and peeling wallpaper. The stench of neglect and desperation hung in the air, suffocating their senses. Without a word, the team pressed forward, their movements synchronized as they cleared each room, their senses on high alert.

Bancroft spotted a family portrait in the corner of the living room, a stark contrast to the desolation surrounding them. It held the picture of a heavily bearded blonde man with a smiling woman beside him and a baby girl passionately clutched in his bulbous arms.

The dog trainer, Ethan, followed Max's keen senses as they navigated the hallways. It was a big building. The atmosphere grew increasingly tense, each step fraught with anticipation. The muffled sound of voices reached their ears, growing louder as they drew closer to their destination.

They reached a closed door, beyond which they sensed the presence of life. Sheriff Mandta raised his hand, signalling the team to prepare for action. Bancroft positioned himself by the door, his heart pounding, his mind focused on the task.

Sheriff Mandta kicked open the door with a nod, and chaos erupted. The two men, their faces contorted with desperation and greed, stood between the rescuers and another woman. Guns were drawn, their barrels gleaming ominously in the dim light. A deadly firefight ensued, the air thick with the acrid scent of gunpowder, as Bancroft and the sheriff's team exchanged gunfire with the captors.

Bancroft moved with the precision of a predator, his training and instincts guiding him through the chaos. He dove behind a piece of furniture, bullets whizzing past, and his senses heightened to the sound of each shot, the flashes of gunfire illuminating the room in fleeting bursts.

Sheriff Mandta, a seasoned lawman, provided crucial support, his voice steady as he barked orders. His team moved with calculated precision, utilizing cover and returning fire, determined to neutralize the threat and rescue Sarah from her captors.

Amidst the chaos, Bancroft caught a glimpse of Sarah, bound and gagged, her eyes wide with fear but brimming with hope. With determination etched on his face, he manoeuvred through the room, evading the onslaught of bullets. Inch by inch, he closed the distance between them, defying the odds and refusing to let the fear consume him.

Bullets whizzed past, smashing into walls and shattering glass, but Bancroft remained firm. His hands trembled with adrenaline and flair as he swiftly freed Sarah from her restraints. With a final tug, the bonds fell away, and he embraced her, offering reassurance during the chaos.

"You're safe, Sarah. I promised him to bring you back alive," Bancroft whispered as the tears from Sarah's sobbing began to wet his shirt.

Outside the room, the firefight raged on, the air punctuated by the staccato of gunfire and the shouts of combat. The sheriff's team pushed forward, their training and resolve shining through the haze of danger. They pressed the attackers back, cornering them desperately for survival.

In a burst of fury and desperation, the captors finally attempted to escape, their backs against the wall. The firefight reached its climax, the air heavy with the weight of their actions. Shots rang out, echoes reverberating through the room until silence finally descended.

Once a prison of despair, the room now served as a sanctuary of freedom. Sarah clung to Bancroft, tears of relief streaming down her face, her faith in humanity restored. As the adrenaline subsided, Bancroft surveyed the aftermath, the room now a tableau of shattered dreams and vanquished threats.

Sheriff Mandta approached, his eyes reflecting a mixture of exhaustion and triumph. "We did it, Bancroft. We got her out."

Bancroft nodded, his gaze lingering on the bruised but resilient woman before him. "We got her back, Sheriff."

The echoes of the firefight faded into the background as they helped Sarah out of the room and into the safety of the waiting authorities. The battle had been won, but the war against the shadows would continue.

As he stepped out of the house, the night air washing over him, Bancroft cast one final glance at the scene of the rescue. The sight of Sarah's freedom filled him with a renewed sense of purpose, propelling him into the darkness that awaited him.

The battle may have been won, but the war against the shadows had only begun.

How many such battles am I supposed to fight?

CHAPTER TWENTY-FOUR

THE BUSTLING CITY STREET of Central Capeton pulsed with life, teeming with people going about their daily routines. Bancroft was among the sea of faces, his keen eyes surveying the urban landscape. For months, he hadn't been to that part of the town. But, the search for clues took him that far. He was to wait for Detective Hunter at an art gallery down the street.

As if summoned by fate, a commotion erupted nearby, catching his attention. A streetwise man darted through the crowd, clutching a stolen bag, while a distressed girl trailed after him, desperation etched across her face.

With determination, Bancroft sprinted into action, his long strides propelling him forward. Weaving through the maze of bodies, he pursued the nimble thief, adrenaline coursing through his veins. The cacophony of bustling streets faded into a background blur as he focused solely on the elusive figure ahead.

The chase led them through narrow alleyways, their footsteps echoing against the walls like the heartbeat of pursuit. The street man displayed uncanny agility, dodging obstacles with acrobatic grace. Bancroft pushed himself to the limits, his relentless pursuit fueled by a desire for justice and the thrill of the chase.

You're not getting away with this! Not today!

As they neared a crowded marketplace, the thief's daring increased. He expertly manoeuvred through the stalls, skillfully eluding Bancroft' grasp. The investigator's frustration grew, but he refused to yield, determined to bring the culprit to justice and recover the stolen belongings.

Suddenly, a burst of speed propelled the street man forward, his movements almost supernatural. He leapt over crates, vaulted past fruit stands, and squeezed through impossibly narrow gaps, leaving a trail of awe and disbelief in his wake. Bancroft matched his every move, their chase escalating into a mesmerizing display of skill and endurance.

Bad meets evil!

With each passing moment, the street man's audacity grew, his confidence spiralling into recklessness. He pushed his luck to the edge, zigzagging through traffic, narrowly avoiding collisions with startled pedestrians. The chaos of the chase painted a vivid portrait of desperation and defiance against the backdrop of the city's rhythm.

But fate has a way of intervening at the most unexpected moments. As the street man careened around a corner, his grip on the stolen bag faltered, and it slipped from his grasp, tumbling to the ground. He hesitated for a fraction of a second, torn between retrieving his ill-gotten gains and continuing his mad escape. Sensing an opportunity, Bancroft seized his chance. Bancroft would have whacked him to the ground if the man had moved a step backwards.

Closing in with newfound determination, Bancroft lunged forward, his hand outstretched, ready to apprehend the thief. But just as he was within inches of capturing his quarry, the street man made a split-second decision. He abandoned the bag, leaving it behind like a relic of his fleeting victory, and darted into the maze of alleyways, disappearing into the town's shadows.

It was the best decision.

Breathing heavily, Bancroft skidded to a stop, his eyes fixed on the abandoned bag. The silence of the aftermath enveloped him, the town's pulse fading into a distant hum. He approached the bag cautiously, his senses alert, his mind racing with possibilities. It held the remnants of the chase — a testament to the fleeting nature of ill-gotten gains and the tenacity of those pursuing justice.

As he inspected the contents, his gaze shifted towards the horizon, the town stretching before him like an endless sky. The chase may have ended for now, but the pursuit of truth and justice remained an eternal flame within his soul. The street man had evaded capture, but his actions had consequences, and Bancroft vowed to ensure that those consequences would find him.

With the stolen bag in hand, Bancroft turned his back on the scene, his resolve undeterred. The chase fueled his determination, igniting a fire guiding his relentless pursuit.

The streets whispered with the echoes of his footsteps as he disappeared into the urban tapestry, ready to continue his quest against the shadows threatening the town's peace.

His phone rang, and he knew he'd have to hurry up.

Detective Hunter was waiting at the gallery!

The atmosphere in the dimly lit room was thick with tension as Detective Christopher Hunter leaned forward, his gaze locked on the club's manager. "You better start talking," he growled, his voice dripping with authority. "We know you're holding something back. Rachel's life is on the line."

The manager, beads of sweat forming on his forehead, shifted uncomfortably in his chair. His eyes darted around the room, seeking an escape route that didn't exist. He knew the stakes were high, and the relentless determination in Christopher's eyes made it clear that he wasn't going to back down.

"I swear, I don't know anything!" the manager stammered, his voice trembling with fear. "Rachel was just a dancer here. I mean a stripper. She didn't tell me anything about what she was involved in."

Christopher's patience wore thin, his frustration boiling beneath the surface. He slammed his hand on the table, causing the manager to flinch. "You expect me to believe that?" he snapped, his voice sharp with accusation. "You run this place. You must know the shit that runs deep down here."

As the interrogation intensified, Detective Elaine Murphy watched silently from the corner of the room, her gaze never wavering. She knew that sometimes a softer approach could yield better results. "Listen to me," she said, her voice calm but firm. "Rachel's life is in danger. If you know anything, now is the time to speak up. We can protect you, but you have to cooperate."

The manager hesitated, his eyes flickering with uncertainty. The weight of the situation pressed upon him, and he knew that his silence could cost Rachel her life. With a deep breath, he finally relented, his words tumbling out in a rush.

"Okay, okay! There was this guy a regular here," the manager admitted, his voice filled with fear and guilt. "He had connections, and he often mentioned some shady business dealings. Rachel seemed to be getting close to him, but I never thought it would lead to something like this."

Detective Hunter's eyes narrowed, his focus sharpening. "What's this guy's name?" he demanded, his voice cutting through the tension.

The manager hesitated momentarily before replying, "His name is Eduardo Ruiz. He's a powerful figure out there..."

"Out where?" Bancroft asked.

"The streets! He operates out of the Westside."

The revelation sent a chill down the detectives' spines. They had finally obtained a lead, a name to pursue. But the road ahead would be treacherous, and they needed to tread carefully.

"We need to find him," Bancroft interjected, his voice filled with determination. "If anyone knows where Rachel is, it's him."

Elaine glanced at Bancroft, a flicker of concern crossing her features. She knew the risks involved in confronting someone as dangerous as Eduardo Ruiz. "He's deadly. He won't give up information easily."

Bancroft nodded, the gravity of the situation weighing heavily upon him. "I understand," he replied, his voice resolute. "But we can't let fear hold us back. Rachel's life is at stake."

Just as they prepared to devise a plan to confront Eduardo Ruiz, a sudden beep interrupted the moment's intensity. Bancroft reached into his pocket and pulled out his phone, his heart beating as he read the message on the screen.

It was a text from Rachel.
His hands trembled with relief and anticipation as he relayed the message to his companions. "We have a breakthrough," he declared, his voice filled with excitement and urgency.

"It's her!" he announced.

The room erupted with a renewed sense of energy and purpose. The text message had injected new life into their investigation, providing them with a tangible lead to follow.

Montebello was the destination, and they knew they had to move quickly.

As they hurriedly prepared to depart, the club's manager looked on with relief and apprehension. "Please, find her," he pleaded, his voice laced with genuine concern. "I didn't realize how dangerous things had become. I never meant for any harm to come to Rachel."

Elaine locked eyes with the manager, her expression softening for a moment. "We'll do everything in our power to bring her back safely," she assured him, her voice filled with compassion. "But you need to cooperate fully. Tell us everything you know, no matter how small. It could make all the difference."

The manager nodded, a glimmer of hope shining in his eyes. "I'll do whatever it takes to make things right," he replied, his voice filled with determination. "Rachel deserves to be saved."

"One more thing," Bancroft halted and turned to the club manager.

"Mention this to no one!"

CHAPTER TWENTY-FIVE

"WELCOME TO MONTEBELLO, Bancroft Logan," the voice over the telephone taunted, its tone dripping with malicious intent. The words sent a chill down Bancroft' spine, a foreboding sense of danger settling in the pit of his stomach. Montebello, a city shrouded in darkness and ruled by criminals, was a treacherous battleground where the rules were twisted and the stakes were high.

In the heart of the vast warehouse, Rachel was bound to a metallic chair, her eyes filled with fear and determination. The abductors had orchestrated this twisted game, their motives veiled in shadows. They needed Bancroft to comply with their demands to ensure Rachel's safety.

It was his only elixir!

Bancroft took a deep breath, his mind focused as he listened to the instructions whispered through the phone. The voice on the other end of the line was relentless, manipulating the chessboard of this dangerous game. To ensure Rachel's survival, he had no choice but to comply.

No tricks.

No games.

Just full loyalty.

Besides a heap of containers, three figures emerged from the darkness. Two burly men and a woman, their presence exuding a menacing aura. The woman, taller than the men and with a punk-like appearance, possessed an athletic build that would rival that of a male gymnast—except for her feminine features, particularly her pronounced breasts.

As Bancroft observed the scene before him, trying to make sense of the twisted game he found himself in, the voice on the phone uttered words that sent a shiver down his spine. Memories long buried resurfaced, reminding him of the darkness he had faced in his past.

"Not everyone deserves a chance!"

The voice's chilling words echoed in Bancroft' mind, stirring memories of past encounters with merciless criminals who had crossed his path. The phrase served as a grim reminder of the ruthless nature of the game he was caught up in. The abductors had chosen him for a reason, and he couldn't help but wonder what sinister purpose lay behind their actions.

Bancroft' gaze narrowed, his determination burning brighter than ever. He would play their game but wouldn't allow them to break him. With Rachel's life hanging in the balance, he steeled himself for what lay ahead, ready to face whatever challenges awaited him.

The voice on the phone continued to issue instructions, each leading Bancroft deeper into the dark, getting him closer to where Rachel was bound. He moved purposefully, and his senses heightened as he navigated the warehouse, following the twisted path before him.

As he neared the trio of abductors, their eyes locked on him, their expressions a mixture of smugness and anticipation. They relished in this twisted game, revelling in their power over Bancroft.

The woman, her punk-like appearance accentuated by her defiant stance, stepped forward with a mocking smile. "It's sad that of all the bravery tales I've heard about, you still played right into the den you were originally meant to be."

"Who are you?"

She chuckled. "I'm what you don't ever wish to encounter. Your harbinger," the woman growled.

"Let her go and do whatever you want!" Bancroft said.

"What a Romeo you are! You think you've got a befitting Juliet, and I guess!" she said amid a loud laugh.

"What do you want?"

"We already have what we want, Bancroft. You're and have always been just a pawn in our game," she sneered, her voice laced with malice. "But don't worry, we'll make it entertaining before the end."

Bancroft' jaw clenched, his muscles taut with tension. He knew he couldn't afford to let their taunts distract him. Every move, every action, had to be calculated with precision.

Bancroft stared back at the woman with a steely resolve, his voice filled with unwavering determination. "You've underestimated me," he retorted, his words cutting through the air. "I'm not just a pawn. I'm the one who will tear down your plans and rescue Rachel."

The trio of abductors exchanged glances, momentarily thrown off by Bancroft' unwavering confidence. The woman's sneer turned into a scowl as she realized that Bancroft was not an opponent to be taken lightly. Or still be underestimated.

The voice over the phone crackled with frustration, a hint of uncertainty seeping through the distorted sound. "You think you can outsmart us, Bancroft?" it hissed. "You're playing a dangerous game."

A defiant smile tugged at Bancroft' lips as he replied, his voice laced with determination. "I've played dangerous games before," he said, his words ringing with conviction. "And I always come out on top."

With that, Bancroft dove into action. The battle for Rachel's life was about to unfold, a showdown between his determination and their cruelty. He moved precisely, using his wit, agility, and years of training to outmanoeuvre the abductors.

Blows were exchanged, the sounds of punches and grunts reverberating through the warehouse. Bancroft fought with a fierce determination, his every move fueled by the love he held for Rachel and the need to bring her back safely.

The abductors fought back, their strength and size giving them an advantage. But Bancroft refused to be deterred, drawing upon his experience and resourcefulness to turn their tactics against them.
In one of his moves, he misstepped, giving the woman a chance to let out a kick right into his face. It was a hard one. One that sent him crashing to the ground in exhaustion.

One of the men held him up. At that point, Bancroft could see his face. He recognized it. The same face broke into the club and squeezed Rachel out.

While Bancroft's legs stood mid-air as the figure left him to hang in the balance, the other drove his hairless head right into Bancroft' midsection.

He fell to the ground in a loud stud, his grunts droning the air. He heard the cock of a gun and then a reecho of the same familiar phrase he heard earlier.

Not everyone deserves a chance!

As Bancroft stood during the aftermath, memories from his past flooded his mind like a relentless torrent sweeping away any semblance of peace. It was a tragic memory…one filled with a tragedy that had shaped him into the man he had become— a man driven by a haunted past.

His brother, once filled with dreams and aspirations, had succumbed to the dark grip of depression. The weight of his struggles eventually led him down a path of addiction until it consumed him entirely. Bancroft had watched helplessly as his brother spiralled deeper into darkness, unable to save him from the clutches of his demons.

But the true depths of the tragedy unfolded when his brother's desperation pushed him to commit an unspeakable act. He had assembled a team of robbers seeking to extort money from their parents. His insane dream of running an illegal arms operation with Russian dealers had consumed him, and he believed his parents held the key to the funds he needed.

Fear, anger, and desperation had clouded his brother's judgment. As he held his father at gunpoint, his father recognized a scar on his upper wrist—a scar that carried the weight of a painful memory. His father called out his name, and in a moment of panic, his brother had made a fateful choice. He pulled the trigger, extinguishing the life of the one who had brought him into this world.

He killed his father.

Their father!

Bancroft' mother, unable to witness the horror that unfolded before her, suffered a heart attack, leaving her lifeless body crumpled on the floor. The Russians, who had forced his brother into this twisted scheme, showed no mercy. They also shot his mother, leaving a trail of devastation in their wake.

They wiped them all!

Leaving nothing behind!

Bancroft had sought justice for his family, Distraught and filled with a thirst for vengeance. The webcams that captured the tragic event had been tampered with, but with his keen eye and relentless determination, Bancroft had discovered the truth within the distorted footage. He saw his brother's face, the one who had betrayed their family.

The one who made him pocket the love of brother could have for another.

Fueled by a sense of righteous anger, Bancroft sought out the Russians who fled the country with the money they had stolen from their father. He knew he had to stop them to prevent any further suffering. It led him to a drug deal with two Spanish teenagers—a desperate attempt to gather the resources needed to confront the criminals who had torn his family apart.

But before the buyers arrived, Bancroft intercepted them. His training as a Navy SEAL had honed his skills, making the confrontation relatively easy. He incapacitated the Spanish teenagers, their lives snuffed out in the blink of an eye, driven by a grim determination.

His brother, shot in the leg, lay there in agony. Bancroft, torn between his desire for revenge and a lingering need for closure, wanted to confront him, to have a final conversation before ending it all. But fate had a different plan.

The SWAT team alerted to the unfolding situation, stormed the scene with tear gas, and chaos ensued. Bancroft was forced to retreat, the brother he so desperately sought to confront taken into custody. He never saw his brother again until he had served his prison term, a broken man consumed by addiction. His brother's life ended tragically, swallowed by the darkness that had haunted him for so long.

And in that moment of despair, Bancroft could still vividly recall the words he uttered to the Spanish teenagers before ending their lives—the same words that echoed through the twisted game he found himself in now:

"Not everyone deserves a chance."

The strange voice on the phone laughed hysterically, its tone filled with a chilling malevolence. It drowned in the darkness that had consumed Bancroft' life, mocking the tragedies that had led him to this point.

"That was where the game all started!" the voice declared, its words laced with sinister amusement. It was a cruel reminder that Bancroft was merely a player in a twisted game, manipulated by forces beyond his control.

Bancroft clenched his fists, his heart heavy with the weight of his past. He was back on his feet now. The game had begun before this warehouse and Rachel's abduction. It was a game playing out in the shadows, and its roots were buried deep in his shattered history.

But as the voice's laughter filled the air, Bancroft knew one thing with unwavering certainty—he would not let this game consume him. The echoes of his past had driven him to this point, but he would rise above the darkness that had plagued his life. Rachel's life depended on it.

Bancroft steeled himself for the challenges ahead with a renewed sense of purpose. The game may have begun, but he was determined to finish it on his terms. He would navigate the treacherous path before him, untangle the webs of conspiracy, and rescue Rachel from the clutches of those who sought to destroy them both.

"What do you want?"

CHAPTER TWENTY-SIX

DETECTIVE HUNTER was finally led into the warehouse. Seeing every sign of a ready battle, they split, their guns on their masks, a feeling of unease settled over them. They knew the game was far from over, and the emptiness of their guns served as a cruel reminder of the danger that lurked in the hall.

Suddenly, a haunting laughter echoed through the air, sending a shiver down their spines. They turned their attention towards the source, their eyes widening in disbelief.

It was Detective Elaine. Her hysterical laughter was filled with a chilling madness. The revelation struck Bancroft like a thunderbolt. Standing beside Elaine, Rachel wore an expression of betrayal mixed with pain. It was then that the puzzle pieces began to fall into place.

The two men and the strange lady who had emerged earlier were also part of this twisted conspiracy. They had been working in tandem, their roles intricately woven into the fabric of Bancroft' life.

But the most shocking revelation came when the voice that had tormented Bancroft over the phone descended upon them. It was Adams Gibson, the Chief of Capeton's PD, who had overseen the investigation that had brought them together.

In a chilling moment, the truth unfolded before them. Those closest to them had orchestrated the intricate web of deceit, betrayal, and revenge. Elaine and Rachel, siblings hidden behind a veil of darkness, had been playing their parts for years.

Elaine's suspension from the Montebello PD had been a calculated move, paving the way for the events leading to this moment. Not even Bancroft nor Detective Hunter knew about her suspension. Not after the letter meant for Montebello PD never got posted.

Rachel, positioned as a honey trap, had ensnared Bancroft in a dangerous game of love and manipulation. "You let love get into your head," Rachel said. "Love that never actually existed."

The actual murderer, the one responsible for the string of deaths that had haunted them, was none other than Kia—the strange, manlike woman who had attacked Bancroft alone and in the presence of Rachel.

"I get sick when I hear you're a Navy SEAL," Kia said. "You move too slow and punch too weakly!"

Bancroft couldn't get his head around what was unfolding before his eyes. He never at any point imagined that the attacker was a woman.

However, the true mastermind behind it all was Detective Elaine herself. She had orchestrated the murders, implanting Otis Crane's DNA at the crime scenes to make Bancroft go in circles and never get anything done!"

As the truth unfolded, each individual took turns revealing their true selves. To Bancroft, nothing sounded so shockingly intriguing as that!

With a cold, calculated gaze, Chief Adams admitted to his role in the conspiracy. The revelation hit Bancroft like a blow to the gut—the chief had just two sons, the very same Spanish teenagers Bancroft had killed years ago in an attempt to protect his family.

"I had two freaking marriages that all failed. One of them gave me," he turned to Elaine and Rachel. "Gave us those boys…but you took them away…you wiped them off the earth," Chief Adams Gibson.

"Eight long years had passed since that fateful day," the chief said. "He spoke with eloquence but his voice held crumbs of pain.

The chief had waited patiently, nurturing his thirst for vengeance. He had used his daughters, Rachel and Elaine, to exact his twisted form of justice.

With Rachel now freed from her restraints, the tension in the warehouse reached its climax. Elaine's eyes filled with a seething hatred for Bancroft reminded Christopher and Bancroft of her training and military background. She had served in the US Army as a captain, honing her skills and cultivating her dark desire to destroy anything and anyone associated with Bancroft Logan.

"I went to battles. I fought in valleys, hills and rainforests to prepare well enough to live my dream. To watch you bleed slowly until life is squeezed out of your lungs."

In a shocking turn of events, Rachel raised the gun she had been given and aimed it at Bancroft' leg. The room fell silent, the moment's weight hanging heavy in the air. It seemed like the end of the line for Bancroft—a final act of betrayal that would seal his fate.

"You must have thought what we shared was love. Was affection. Was I giving it my all? And I did give it my all. We needed the right script after you killed our brothers and spared yours. We needed a perfect crime. We needed the silent death. It took us years. Quite a long time to wait for demand and at least it came," Rachel explained. She shot Bancroft in the shoulder.

"Note my precision, Bancroft. It took me years to hone it. Of course. Just for you!"
She'd recall all of it.

The road to her crazy shooting performance.

As the buzzer sounded, signalling the start of the challenge, she recalled how John swiftly drew his pistol from his holster and took aim at the first target. He squeezed the trigger with calm focus and well-practised technique, sending a round straight to the target's head. The shot connects with precision, resulting in an immediate hit.

Without wasting any time, John transitioned to the next target. His muscle memory and extensive training kick in, allowing him to acquire the new target quickly and maintain his accuracy. He fires another round, and the second target is hit in the head.

John continued this rapid and precise engagement, shifting his aim from target to target. His movements are fluid and efficient, maximizing his time while maintaining accuracy. With each shot, he showcased his exceptional marksmanship.

As the two-minute mark approached, John fired his fifth and final shot, striking the head of the last target. The challenge ended with impressive speed, accuracy, and control.

For months, she watched him do that. In her sixth month, she was already at ten headshots in two minutes at a 50-meter distance.

She enjoyed it.

For the first time, she used it on someone. The same person who made her ever think of going down that lane.

As Bancroft struggled to hoist his frame, Rachel cleared her throat. "I warned you with every fibre of my being. I wanted the best for you and all that you cared about. You wouldn't listen. I killed him. The court clerk. Scot Palmer. He jailed my Cuban left-wing man and felt he could walk around like some innocent bag of holiness. The boy on the train saw more than he had to! I didn't mean this, but she did."

Bancroft could feel his hair rising. The revelation was getting too intense for him to take in.
"Why did you take their lives, Bancroft?" she asked, closing in on them.

"I didn't intend to leave a life behind. The gasses took me unaware completely off balance. He got lucky!"

"Why would the lucky one be your brother?

"He was never my brother. I'd treated him even worse. He lost that title when he shot the person that mattered most to us."

The more Rachel got closer, Bancroft jolted away. He knew she was up for more.

Meanwhile, Detective Hunter, always vigilant and perceptive, saw through the plan before it unfolded. He had noticed Elaine's manipulation from the beginning, the deliberate act of removing the gun from Bancroft' pillow, and the intentional killing of the nurse.

With a quick punch of his watch, the area around the containers erupted in a fiery explosion, chaos consuming the space. The blast forfeited Kia and the two men, leaving them incapacitated.

Amidst the chaos, a sniper's bullet found its mark, taking down Rachel from a vantage point above the warehouse. The realization of her betrayal pierced Bancroft' heart, but he knew he had to press on. She fell to the ground as the bullet hit her upper arm.

It never had to be a headshot!

Detective Elaine, wounded but still dangerous, engaged Bancroft in a gritty, no-holds-barred fight. The room became a battlefield, their movements fueled by hatred and desperation. Blow after blow, and they fought with an intensity that matched the flames of their twisted past.

She fought like a berserker.

He fought back like a famished jaguar.

Bancroft' voice cut through the chaos, filled with determination. "You betrayed me, Elaine. But I won't let you destroy everything I've fought for!"

Elaine's eyes burned with ruthless resolve. "You never understood, Bancroft. You were always the pawn, the means to an end. It's time to pay for your sins!"

Their fists collided, the impact reverberating through the air. Each blow was laced with the weight of their shared history, the culmination of years of deceit and manipulation.

As Bancroft dodged Elaine's powerful strikes, his voice rang out with an unwavering determination. "I may have been a pawn in your twisted game, but I refuse to let you win. I will bring justice to those you've harmed!"

With each punch, each kick, the intensity of their fight escalated. Blood stained their faces, their bodies aching with exhaustion. But Bancroft' spirit remained unbroken, his resolve unwavering.

Finally, a moment of vulnerability presented itself. Elaine's guard momentarily dropped, and Bancroft seized the opportunity. With a lightning-fast move, he disarmed her, their gazes locked in a battle of wills.

Bancroft' voice was filled with a mix of sadness and resolve. "I gave you chances, Elaine. But you chose darkness."

In a final act of desperation, Elaine lunged forward, attempting to regain control. But Bancroft, fueled by a fierce determination, evaded her attack. He raised his gun, his hands steady despite the fatigue coursing through his veins.

Elaine's eyes widened, the realization of her impending fate etched across her face. "You can't do it, Bancroft. We were family once!"

His voice was firm, tinged with a hint of sorrow. "Family doesn't betray each other, Elaine. This is where it ends."

With a heavy pull of the trigger, a single gunshot shattered the silence. Elaine's body crumpled to the floor, her life extinguished. The room fell into a heavy silence, the weight of their shared history settling around Bancroft.

Meanwhile, Detective Hunter faced off against Chief Adams, both men locked in a battle that symbolized the culmination of their shared history. Blow after blow, and they fought, each driven by their motives. Hunter's resilience and training kept him one step ahead, gradually weakening the chief until he could no longer stand.

Hunter brought the chief to his knees with a final, decisive strike. His voice echoed with a mix of determination and fatigue. "Your twisted game ends here, Adams. The price you've paid for revenge has left a trail of destruction."

Chief Adams' voice was filled with bitter defiance. "I will never regret what I've done. You don't understand the pain I've endured!"

Detective Hunter's voice softened, ebbed with a fake hint of empathy. "I may not understand your pain, but I've seen the consequences. Revenge only leads to darkness."

As the chief crumbled to the floor, defeated, the sirens grew louder, heralding the arrival of the SWAT team from Montebello PD. The warehouse was now a battlefield littered with the remnants of a twisted plot.

Bancroft, bloodied and battered, gazed at the chaos around him. The truth had been laid bare, and the darkness that had haunted him for years was finally brought to light. He knew the wounds inflicted on his soul would take time, but knowing that justice had prevailed provided solace.

Bancroft turned his attention to the fallen as the SWAT team secured the area and apprehended the remaining threats. His eyes lingered on the lifeless bodies of Elaine and the half-dead Rachel, the sisters who had become entangled in a web of deceit and revenge. The weight of their choices and the tragic path they had followed weighed heavy on his heart.

"Rest on", Bancroft whispered, his voice filled with sadness and regret. "May you find the solace that eluded you in life."

Amid the wreckage, Detective Hunter approached Bancroft, his face etched with exhaustion and a sombre determination. Their eyes met, and a shared understanding passed between them. They had faced the darkest corners of their past and emerged on the other side, forever changed.

"We did what we had to do," Detective Hunter said, his voice filled with resignation. "Sometimes, the lines between right and wrong become blurred."

Bancroft nodded, his gaze focused on the aftermath of their harrowing journey. "We may carry the scars of our past, but we can't let them define us."

A profound silence settled over the scene as they stood in the warehouse, surrounded by the remnants of the conspiracy that had ensnared them.

The echoes of their past seemed to dissipate, replaced by a flicker of hope for a brighter future.

Will crimes make it bright enough?

EPILOGUE

"I DIDN'T KNOW THAT CRIMINALS have the best love stories! Did you?" Bancroft spoke mockingly, his voice echoing through the sterile walls of the interrogation room.

Rachel, dressed in the generic orange prison uniform, glared at him with fiery eyes, her anger palpable. The years had not been kind to her, and the weight of their shared history lingered heavily between them. She took on a different look, although not wholly shedding off the beauty that once stunned Bancroft to a stupor.

"Love story?" she scoffed, her voice dripping with bitterness. "There was never any love between us, Bancroft. Just chaos and destruction," she cursed.

Bancroft smiled. "That doesn't matter anymore. Doesn't it?"

She glanced across the counter as if she was about to tell him what the guards were never supposed to hear. "What are you here, you asshole? To mock me?"

"Not like I won't if I wanted to! But you know why I'm here, Rachel!"

"To hell with your assumptions, Bancroft. Cut to the chase."

"Where's the baby?"

Rachel laughed hard. So hard that the guard at the door got startled but Bancroft signaled that all was well. "You dared to ask about a child? Why does it matter now?"

Bancroft leaned back in his chair, a mocking smile on his lips. "Oh, Rachel, did you think I would be interested in your spawn? The offspring of deceit and treachery? I'm just curious if you had the guts to go through with it or if it was all a desperate ploy."

Rachel's face contorted with anger, and she kicked out at him, her foot connecting with the table between them. "You heartless bastard! You think this is some sick game?"

"What then is it?"

"I'll never forgive you, Bancroft. And when I leave this prison, I'll make you pay."

"You need therapy, Rachel. That's all you need!"

"Fuck you and your god-damned therapy, you asshole. I'll make you pay, Bancroft. For the pain. All of it!"

Bancroft chuckled darkly, the sound filling the room. "Make me pay, Rachel? How amusing. You were just a pawn in a larger game, a casualty of your family's web of lies. Don't delude yourself into thinking you had any power over me."

Rachel's eyes burned with rage, her gaze fixed on Bancroft. "You think you're so clever, don't you? Enjoy your victory while it lasts. I'll find a way to make you regret this, Bancroft."

Bancroft leaned forward, his voice dripping with condescension. "Regret? Oh, Rachel, I thrive on regret. It fuels me, and propels me forward. But you, my dear, will be a forgotten memory in the grand scheme."

Their words hung in the air, the bitter exchange marking the end of their twisted dance. Rachel seethed with anger, her face flushed with hatred and determination. Bancroft wallowed in the chaos he had unleashed, basking in his perceived superiority.

As the guards outside the room prepared to escort Rachel back to her cell, Bancroft watched her retreating figure with a triumphant smirk. Their paths had converged and clashed, leaving a trail of ruin in their wake.

"I look forward to it, Rachel," Bancroft said, his voice dripping with mockery. "But don't forget; I always seem to have the last laugh."

Rachel's eyes narrowed, her voice laced with venom. "You may think you've won, Bancroft, but the game isn't over. I'll find a way to expose your true nature, to tear down the facade you've built."

Bancroft laughed, the sound filled with cold, calculated amusement. "Expose me? Rachel, you underestimate the lengths I will go to protect my secrets if at all I've got any. But by all means, try your best. It will be a delight to watch you fail."

As the door closed behind Rachel, Bancroft was left alone in the stark room, a satisfied smile playing on his lips. He had achieved his goal of unravelling her family's secrets, revelling in the destruction he had brought upon them.

In the depths of his soul, Bancroft waxed in the power he held over Rachel. The prison walls may have confined her physically, but the emotional prison they shared was far more suffocating.

As he left the interrogation room, he knew he had emerged as the victor in their twisted game.

That joy that comes with victory is an unsung therapy!

The End!

Bolted UPRIGHT
VAULTED) ofc
LAUNCHED) off
JUMPED
Leapt
Recoiled
Rocked
shuddered
TWITCHED)
CONTORTED
BLACK OUT
2ND JULY
1968
Printed in Great Britain
by Amazon
11:40 AM

25729442R00172